DANGER'S HUNT

A HOLLY DANGER NOVEL:
BOOK FIVE

AMANDA CARLSON

DANGER'S HUNT

A HOLLY DANGER NOVEL: BOOK FIVE

ISBN-13: 978-1986387903
ISBN-10: 1986387909

OTHER BOOKS BY AMANDA CARLSON

Jessica McClain Series:
Urban Fantasy

BLOODED
FULL BLOODED
HOT BLOODED
COLD BLOODED
RED BLOODED
PURE BLOODED
BLUE BLOODED

Sin City Collectors:
Paranormal Romance

ACES WILD
ANTE UP
ALL IN

Phoebe Meadows:
Contemporary Fantasy

STRUCK
FREED
EXILED

Holly Danger:
Futuristic Dystopian

DANGER'S HALO
DANGER'S VICE
DANGER'S RACE
DANGER'S CURE
DANGER'S HUNT

For Bridget.

The best writing companion a girl could ask for.

Chapter 1

"Going alone is too risky," Bender argued. "You heard Reed when we gave him Babble. He said his militia is one hundred and seventy-six strong, and Tillman, an imminent threat in his own right, has another thirty at least." Bender had his shoulder braced against the wall. We were all convened in the basement of the government building we'd recently taken over, the whir of the medi-pod churning at a steady rate.

Mary had been in there for at least two hours.

I stood in the middle of the room, arms crossed, facing off with my crew about the dangerous journey I was about to embark on, whether they liked it or not. "I'm not backing down on this. If we don't take them by surprise, we lose any chance of getting Case out of there." Backing down was not going to happen. Daze stood near me, sniffling, still blaming himself for Case's capture. It seemed Reed, our unwilling Bureau of Truth prisoner and informant, had been implanted with a tracking device. The militia had lost his signal when he'd entered the barracks, but had lain in wait until Case arrived. By the time I'd gotten there, it was already too late.

"This is my fault," Daze cried miserably. "I'll go with Holly."

I settled a hand on his shoulder. "No one's going with me except Maisie. She's all I need. And if I don't leave soon, Case could be dead by the time I arrive." My gaze trailed from Lockland to Darby, landing on Bender. Ned sat in a chair by the medi-pod, but he wasn't part of this discussion. "They have just over an hour head start as it stands right now. If I move soon, I'll be right behind them. Maisie can help with the rest. She'll be able to locate Case's signature, differentiating it from everyone else's. This is not war. This is me sneaking in and grabbing Case before they can harm him or worse. That's it."

"It's not going to be that simple, and you know it," Lockland retorted. "They're going to have that place on lockdown. They have access to tech we know nothing about. From what you told me from your view in the sky when you and Case were flying to the South, it's a large concrete structure that very well might be impenetrable."

"I never said it would be easy. And nothing is impenetrable, especially with the right gear," I said. "I'm the best chance Case has, and we all know it." Lockland's face was set. "How about this? If Maisie can't find a way in with an expected greater-than-fifty-percent success rate, I'll come back and we'll come up with a new plan. You have my word." We'd found that Maisie had the capacity to calculate strategic odds when it came to mission operations. She was military grade, after all.

"Fifty percent?" Darby balked from his position next to the machine. "I was thinking more like eighty-seven. Why would you risk your life on a fifty percent chance of success?"

"I said greater than fifty," I replied. "I have to account for the fact Maisie will underestimate my skill level. She's a computer. She's going to give me her recommendation based on the combat success rates of an average soldier in her sixty-plus-year-old database. That's not me." I took a step forward. "Listen, I'm going. We can argue about this, but it's only going to waste time. I'm not changing my mind. Case would do the same for me. Hell—any of you would. If I'd been taken, you'd all come after me."

Bender shook his head. "I don't like it. I say one of us goes with you. You're going to need backup."

"No," I said. "The only thing working in our favor is stealth. More than one person and we lose that. Don't forget they have access to live video. I'm planning on sneaking in on the sly, not announcing myself. Maisie will be able to detect threats. I can do this, but I do it with the status reader alone."

Lockland gave me a long look. Then he gave a single nod. "Fine. I can see there's no changing your mind. But the expected success rate, according to Maisie, has to be greater than sixty percent."

"Fifty-five," I countered.

He gave me a hard look. "Sixty."

"Fine," I grumbled. "Then I'll just bring enough firepower with me so that Maisie ups the odds—"

The medi-pod slowed, a green light flickering from the readout.

Anxious to see if Mary was all right, we all converged next to Darby, Lockland and Bender behind me, Daze squeezing in front.

Green was good. At least, I hoped it was.

"What does it say?" Daze asked, his voice conveying our concern. "Is she going to be okay?"

"The preliminary diagnostics look encouraging," Darby replied. "It says eighty percent of the nucleotides have been repaired and are now functioning. Her liver and brain activity are almost normal."

A muffled sound came from inside.

"Darb, open it," I prodded. "She's awake."

The lid on this medi-pod wasn't all glass, like some of the others, so we couldn't see her. Flustered, Darby fumbled with the latch a few times before he managed to get the lid lofted.

I leaned over, Daze next to me, Ned peering down from the other side.

Mary blinked up at us. "Where am I? And…who are you?"

"I'm Holly," I said. "This is Daze. And this is Darby." My head bobbed toward Darby, who had gone temporarily nonverbal. "The guys behind me are Lockland and Bender." I gestured across the pod. "You should know Ned. You guys were neighbors, or so we heard. We're the ones who put you in here. How do you feel?"

She appeared confused, which was to be expected. She'd been out of it for a few weeks. "Am I…okay? My limbs feel heavy, and my brain…feels scrambled." She lifted her hands and cautiously patted the top of her head and face, checking everything out.

I glanced at Darby, who cleared his throat. "Yes, you're okay. According to the readout, you're actually doing very well," he confirmed. "Your DNA was altered by the drug Plush, but this medi-pod was designed to fix it through magnetic refraction. It seems to be doing its job."

"Plush?" She gasped, struggling to sit up. Darby hastily reached out and grasped her shoulders to help. Once she was sitting, her eyes fluttered shut as she brought both index fingers up to her temples. "I was infected with Plush? Is that what you're telling me?"

"Yes, and it's all my fault," Ned gushed in a sorrow-filled voice. "You came outside to talk to me, and Dill grabbed you before I could stop him. It all happened so fast. I'm sorry."

Mary dropped her fingers. "I remember him. He was nasty. He pulled my hair."

Ned nodded. "He took out the dart before I knew what was happening."

Mary reached out, patting Ned on the arm. "It's

okay, I don't blame you. You've always been kind to me, Ned." Her hands clutched the sides of the machine as her gaze drifted across the room. The wall she was looking at had been partially destroyed by a hydro-bomb that Bender had rigged when we'd entered the building. "It looks like something happened here. Does that mean this Dill guy is gone?"

I grinned. I liked Mary already. She was bouncing back with strength. "The wall and Dill are not connected, but I did have the pleasure of giving him a radium ball. He's not going to come looking for you."

Mary made a move to climb out of the pod, but Darby halted her progress with a soft touch. "I'm afraid the healing is going to take a bit longer," he said, his voice gentle. "According to the diagnostics, you're supposed to have another treatment immediately following the ingestion of food and water. Your hydration and nutrient levels are too low to continue. The medi-pod still has work to do, but it will operate more efficiently once you have adequate sustenance."

I spun Daze around by his shoulders. "Go upstairs and see what they have in the form of protein cakes and water. There's a room with a cooling unit on the first floor. Watch yourself." We'd already checked for any threats upstairs, as had Maisie, but one could never be too careful.

Daze nodded, ducking under us and taking off toward the steel steps that would lead him to the main level.

Mary watched him go, realizing for the first time

that we were in a basement of some kind. "What is this place?"

"We're in a building in Government Square," Lockland answered. "We took it over a few hours ago. Our first priority once we arrived was to get you inside this machine, which we did."

"I didn't know there was a medi-pod that could do such a thing," she said. "I'm extremely grateful to you all." She placed a palm over her heart. "Thank you for helping me."

"We didn't know for sure that it existed until a few days ago," I said. There would be time later to fill her in on everything that had happened, including our journey down South, once she was fully healed. "We're thrilled it worked on you, and we're equally optimistic it will work on others."

Daze came buzzing back down the steps with the goods in hand. Ned stepped in front of him, and Daze transferred the protein cake and a cup of water. Ned dutifully brought them to Mary's side and gave them to her. Rather than all of us standing over her watching her eat, we retreated to give her some space.

Bender said in a low voice, "She seems back to normal."

"She does," I said. "It's amazing and such a relief." Now that we knew the medi-pod worked, my mind spun with all the potential things it could do. Coupled with tranq darts and Quell, we'd be able to get seekers in here one by one. It would be a long process, but we could actually cure people.

Lockland pulled a timepiece out of his pocket. “When are you planning to leave?” he asked.

“In the next ten minutes,” I answered.

“If I thought one of us could do a better job,” Lockland said, “I’d send him instead.”

I crossed my arms, giving him a look. “Is that supposed to be a compliment? Because if it is, your delivery sucks.”

“It’s a fact,” he replied, unmoved. “When it comes to making split decisions, you excel. You think twice as fast on your feet as most. If someone in our crew was more suited for this, it would serve Case better to send him instead.” He shrugged. “But you’re the right choice.”

“Case said the same thing not too long ago,” I muttered. “But when he said it, it actually *sounded* like a compliment.”

Lockland grunted. “You’re the outskirt’s best chance for survival, but that doesn’t mean we like it. You’re flying into an incredibly dangerous situation, where the odds of you dying are higher than you living.”

“Not if I stick to the sixty percent,” I said. “With Maisie in my pocket, those are comfortable odds. I’ve already stocked up on supplies.” I’d hastily packed everything I could cram into Luce in less than fifteen minutes. “I’m hitting the barracks for batteries on the way, but that’s my only stop.” The militia had been so intent on grabbing Case, they hadn’t even bothered to do a thorough sweep of the barracks. Daze had been locked in the back room—a room full of enough batteries to power the entire city for a year—and they hadn't investigated. It was poor planning on their part, but lucky for us. I'd need those batteries to keep Luce powered. Getting stuck in the Outskirts wasn't happening. I had no idea how long the rescue operation was going to take, so being prepared was essential.

Bender rubbed the back of his neck, a gesture he made when he was agitated. "We need a deadline," he growled. "If we don't hear from you in two days, we come after you."

"A deadline is good, but we have no way to communicate," I said. "We can't risk conversing on any open airwaves. They monitor the bandwidths down there." I set my hand on his forearm. "I'm coming back. I promise. Once I get Case, and we check in with the scientists and make sure everybody is safe, we'll head back here."

Bender, my mentor and the closest thing to a father I'd ever had, shook his head slowly. "Since we can't communicate, take a tracker. We can locate you with that up to thirty kilometers. That's close enough. Two days from now, Lockland, Daze, and I land outside Walt's dome in the mover drone and wait to pick up your signal. Maisie should be able to detect us on your end. If we don't hear from you, we head to the militia base and bring that motherfucker down."

I glanced at Lockland, who nodded his agreement. "There's no other way to know if you've been taken or killed," he said. "We do it Bender's way." He shot a furtive glance at Daze, who was chatting with Mary like they were old friends. The kid had that effect on people. "Daze will be agitated while you're gone. Knowing we're planning to meet up will take his mind off the situation. He can help us determine the right location to land outside the tribe once we get there, since we can't fly directly in without the risk of triggering their bombs. We'll plan on hugging the coast. We wait six hours once we set down. If we don't hear from you, we head to the militia. But we won't blow it up until we know if you're dead or alive."

"That's a nice, comforting thought," I said. "Except I'm not going to be dead. Neither is Case." That was, if I had anything to say about it. "The plan works for me. There's a good chance the militia will seek out the small tribe with the scientists after I break Case out, if they haven't already. They'll need to gather more troops to take to the city. Up until now, they've been trying to negotiate, but my bet is they take it by force. If they find out what the tribe has been harboring all this time, the battle will intensify. We have to protect that at all costs. Having you guys there is the right choice."

Lockland brought his head down. "It's a plan."

Chapter 2

"Why are goodbyes so hard?" I grumbled.

Maisie replied, her voice issuing out of the smooth polymer egg with her perfect computer-modulated inflection, "Human emotion, when you are dealing with separation from loved ones, can cause a strong reaction in one's state of well-being—"

"Got it," I said, cutting her off. "Thanks for the explanation. That was a rhetorical question, by the way. No need to answer those."

I'd just taken off from the barracks. Luce was packed with everything I could think of, including six batteries, which would be enough to power this craft for at least five years, if not longer. Lockland had insisted I take the barrel laser we'd used while breaking into the government building, as well as a reflective suit, which was capable of redirecting laser fire back at the shooter. The effect wasn't strong enough to kill, like the super-reflective pure fire suits, unless the laser was shot at close range. But wearing it had saved my life a time or two. It was one of our prized possessions.

"I'm familiar with rhetorical questions," Maisie replied. "But your voice did not contain the appropriate cadence or inflection to qualify as such."

I lifted a single eyebrow at the egg, which I had stationed in a groove of the console next to me. She was almost like a person, except not, since she was an inanimate object. I shook my head as I continued to pilot Luce south. We'd be in the air for at least four hours. "You know," I told her, "I'm not sure I trust your authority on human-voice inflections. Not every human sounds the same. We all have our own quirky nuances. That particular question I uttered was rhetorical, but it was also coupled with sarcasm." And a little sadness. Daze had tried to keep it together during our final goodbyes, but he'd made me feel like I was abandoning him without ever voicing a single word of complaint.

His tears and stricken expression had said it all.

He knew this mission was life or death for Case, and the kid blamed himself for what had happened, so he understood I had to go. But that didn't make it any easier. Daze also believed that if Case hadn't taken the time to secure him in the back room, Case would've been able to fight off his kidnappers.

While this might've been true, it was a more likely scenario that Daze would've been taken as well—if not outright killed. The outskirt had saved his life.

From the sounds of it, after I'd calmed the kid down enough to hear the whole story, there had been at least three or four crafts full of Tillman's men. Although the kid hadn't heard any names, I assumed these men belonged to Tillman, who, according to Reed, seemed like the one in charge of all the militia's tactical decisions.

"I will update my references on rhetorical questions to include sarcasm," Maisie asserted. "Even though there was little to no sarcasm detected." Her multicolored lights blinked around the craft, enhancing her point with a subtle mock.

I chuckled. "Are you implying my use of sarcasm was *inadequate*?"

"In the first statement, yes. But now," she answered, "the sarcasm is duly noted."

Grinning, I angled Luce west.

It was going to be a long flight, but at least I had intelligent company to banter with. My goal was to retrace the flight Case and I had taken not so long ago, but it was going to be difficult, because I hadn't been piloting for the first four hours of that trip, and we'd been flying in Seven, not Luce. I had no flight recorder to rely on.

"Maisie," I ordered, getting back to business, "if you can, I need you to access your database from the time when Daze set you free." The kid had somehow managed to activate Maisie to think for herself on that journey. It'd happened right around the time we'd spotted the militia base. "Remember, you informed us about the pulse storm, and shortly after that, we flew over a militia base. You detected a craft following us. Do you have a record of that?"

"Of course," she replied. "I am programmed to remember every encounter."

"Great." With relief, I added, "I need that location. Where the pulse storm began is close enough." I would have to be watchful in my approach, landing well before we reached the headquarters and going in on foot.

Maisie's lights blinked around, this time in an unmocking way, which was easy to see since it was dark outside the craft. Our perpetually occluded sun had set an hour ago. "I have secured a longitudinal and latitudinal record," she said.

That was fast.

But knowing those coordinates wouldn't help me, since to use them, the craft would need to access satellite data that did not exist any longer. "Latitude and longitude won't help," I told her. "I'm going to need you to give me verbal directions. As in, head south thirty kilometers and then turn west for forty-five more."

"I can do that," she said. "For efficiency purposes, if I synced with your flight recorder, I could input the data directly."

"You can do that?" I asked, surprised. I had no idea.

"Yes. Although this craft itself is ancient by modern standards," she said, "its technology has been updated. Your control panel contains AI-compatible software, which is a surprise, but not unwelcome."

"It's not *ancient.*" I snorted, feeling slighted on Luce's behalf, even though this craft had originally been my grandfather's. Being an A class dronecraft, it'd been one of the first off the assembly lines, making it at least seventy-five years old. My ancestors had previously utilized hovercrafts. Hovercrafts had a max altitude of five meters and were boxy and inefficient for long flights. But once the new and improved dronecrafts were engineered, they'd been mass-produced for public consumption. "It's worn in…and comfortable. Like synthetic leather after a year of use. Or sleeping pods, once they've calculated your contours."

"I detect defensiveness in your response," Maisie said. "I will attribute it to your fondness for this craft, which is apparent and well-placed. Subsequent dronecraft models would not have held up as long after prolonged use. Being the first craft manufactured, the A1's engineering safety factor was set higher than in subsequent models. They were constructed with the strongest latticed graphene available. Later models reduced the airframe structural requirements as they added crash-prevention technology, such as air bubbles and parachutes."

I peered at the egg. It was surreal to have so much knowledge so close to me at all times. I wasn't sure I'd ever get used to it. And the way Maisie spoke—it was as if the distant past had happened only yesterday.

She was right about the safety features on personal dronecraft. As time went on and technology advanced, life-saving measures were integrated into all crafts, mandated by law. But they seldom functioned now. Most features required yearly maintenance, especially finicky air bubbles, which were meant to enclose the craft in a silicone aerogel that formed and hardened instantly before impact. Aerogel required a chemical reaction, and most of the chemicals necessary had long since dried up.

"Luce has a parachute," I told her. I maintained it fairly regularly, but I'd never needed to use it, so I actually had no idea if it worked. Last I checked, there were no obvious holes. "This was my grandfather's craft. He took great pains to keep her in good condition, replacing panels when necessary and adding safety features, like the parachute. Bender is the one who upgraded the tech."

"Yes, it seems Bender is talented at fixing things," she said, surprising me. "The circuit boards integrated into your dash have been fused together with parts from three separate crafts. It is an ingenious arrangement. At the time of my creation, nothing like this existed, because before disaster struck, if the panel had malfunctioned, it would have been replaced by an exact replica made by the manufacturer."

"It must be strange for you to take in our world now. It can't really match what's in your database."

"I am fortunate that my integrated software program has what's called Disaster Protocol, which automatically enacts if more than forty percent of my data does not compute with the environment around me. It activated within the first thirty minutes."

I whistled low. "The military thought of everything."

"I would not be much help if a cataclysmic event occurred and I could not adapt," she replied. "My interface was designed at the highest intelligence levels."

"Were they expecting the apocalypse when they made you?" I figured that was unlikely. History noted that the meteor that decimated our planet was initially identified when it collided with an asteroid a short time before it impacted the moon and broke into three pieces, each of which crashed into Earth's surface.

Maisie replied, "It is unknown what they were expecting. Nothing is notated in my database. Disaster Protocol is a standard program, detailing the outcomes of every conceivable event, including, but not limited to, earthquakes, cyclones, tornadoes, tsunamis, volcanoes, and meteor strikes, as well as man-made events, such as nuclear detonations and war, and other unlikely scenarios, such as an alien incursion."

"You're programmed to deal with extraterrestrials?" I chuckled. The military really had thought of everything. "I have a hard time believing anything exists out there, but that's mostly because none of us have ever seen past the clouds with our own eyes."

Maisie's lights began to blink sporadically, morphing suddenly to white as she projected something onto the ceiling and windshield of the craft. "Our solar system is here." A tiny pinpoint of light above my head flickered. It was full of impossibly small stars. She enlarged the projection. "The odds of other planetary life existing are two-point-four to one." The display began to rotate.

"That's incredible," I said as teensy galaxy upon teensy galaxy passed by my line of vision. "The details are so intricate. They actually look like images I've seen. How are you doing that?"

The projection coalesced, and a graphic of Earth landed in the middle of the windshield, spinning slowly. "I have the ability to amplify images, though unlike a hologram program, I am limited to 2-D."

"Don't be too hard on yourself," I said with an awestruck tone in my voice. "This is fantastic. Can you project anything that's in your database?"

"Of course," she confirmed.

"Can you show me the sun?"

A second later, a roiling orb of yellow and orange swirling light hit the windshield. I had to squint because it was so bright. "That's not a picture," I breathed. "I can actually see the gases moving inside."

"This is a moving, pixelated image, formatted for quick viewing. I thought you would enjoy it."

"I do. It's amazing. What else can you do?" I asked.

"I am programmed in four thousand and forty-two languages. I can replay audio of historical events. I can calculate complex equations instantly. I can—"

"Wow, okay. That's more than enough for now," I said, interrupting. "Instead, how about we upload those coordinates into the flight recorder? I'm going to have to make a decision fairly quickly on which way to direct Luce."

"I will require assistance to complete the task," she said.

"What kind of assistance?" I asked, confused.

"My lifecable must be inserted into the dash. There is a small panel located on my underside. Although I can detect and read software remotely, for technology such as that used by this craft, I must be connected physically."

I reached over and picked her up, turning the shell over in my hand. "Lifecable, huh? I don't see a panel."

"It's seamlessly integrated," she replied. The hum of her voice made the polymer vibrate slightly. "Place your fingertip against the bottom. I will detect the heat and open."

I peeled off a glove with my teeth and did as instructed.

Sure enough, a small square slid open with a quiet *schick.* I pressed my shoulder light on to get a better view. A small cable was coiled inside, no more than a few centimeters long. "I don't think I can get your lifecable out of such a tiny opening without damaging—"

A moment later, the cable breached the panel on its own, exposing a standard nine-pronged nano connector, a quarter of the size of my fingernail. Our ancestors had perfected standardization across tech. This plug-in allowed old and new technology to integrate without issue. "Insert my lifecable into your dash's system. I detect three entry points. Use the one nearest the flight data recorder. You must remove a panel to access it."

I knew Luce inside and out. Back before the dark days, her dashboard would've lit up with all kinds of gadgets that relied on satellite and other remote-access programs to operate, including a flight screen. But ever since I'd owned her, most of those components had remained dark. I removed the panel Maisie had referred to, exposing a nano receptacle, and directed Maisie's lifecable into it.

Once connected, Maisie's lights began to flicker, and the previously defunct viewing screen blinked to life for the first time.

As I watched in fascination, numbers scrolled across the liquid crystal screen, accompanied by fleeting images of topography. Everything was moving too fast for me to get an accurate read on our location.

Just as quickly, it stopped, homing in on a location that seemed familiar.

I leaned up in my seat. "That's it, the building we're looking for. It's the one in the middle." I tapped the screen, and the picture enlarged. "Most of the other structures around it are gone." The photo was an aerial graphic, likely taken by satellite long ago. "Do you have any information about this particular site?"

Maisie hung from my dash, snapped in by her lifecable, lights blinking. "The data attributed to the picture states that the target was a medical facility that specialized in the manufacturing and treating of limb defects."

"Limb defects?"

"Yes, humans frequently lost limbs in pedestrian accidents involving public transportation or extreme sporting. This facility developed and fit intelligent 3-D printed bionics onsite and trained patients to use them."

I nodded. "Now that you mention it, I do remember reading about public transportation being prone to accidents. Once everything became automated, and before all the kinks were worked out, there were spates when systems failed on a regular basis. They blamed hackers at the time, but it was never resolved, according to the information left behind. As for extreme sporting, I'd like to see those adventurers try to swing on a cable in the rain fifty stories up with no landing aids strapped to their backs. There's no need for a limb center now. You either survive, or you don't. No second chances." The flight recorder beeped, keeping me on track, and I angled Luce in the direction indicated on the screen. "I guess it makes sense that the militia would make their headquarters there. The building was probably stocked with multiple bio-printers, beds, and basic medical supplies, not to mention medi-pods to keep people relatively healthy." We already knew from Reed that the militia flew people who needed critical care to the medi-pod we were using to fix Mary, as it was fueled by a fusion reactor strong enough to heal desperate injuries.

"That is a possibility," Maisie said. "Or it could be its proximity to the weapons facility."

Chapter 3

"There's a weapons facility nearby?" I asked.

"Yes. According to the data, it produced class A military-grade weapons. Both buildings are located inside a Manufacturing Mecca, which is an area of land dedicated to the making and producing of goods. The structures are clustered close together on purpose to facilitate ease of transport throughout the country. Industrial-sized magnetic-levitation trains converged at their center." Her lights spun in an arc, then disappeared. "You can remove me now. My upload is complete."

I reached over and unplugged her, watching as the tiny cable retracted on its own and the secret door slid shut. "I've heard of Manufacturing Meccas," I said, setting her back on the console. "I've just never seen evidence of one before. The government was heavily involved in their evolution."

"That is correct. Meccas were government-sponsored, and the land was tax-free. There were quite a few throughout the country, but this was one of the largest. Any consumer, from anywhere in the country, could request a high-demand item to be delivered into their hands within minutes or hours from these various locations."

"Wow." I whistled. "Instant gratification was big business."

"This particular mecca earned a combined $3.7 trillion per month."

I could not even begin to fathom coin like that.

The coin we traded now was left over from an era when most people used credit uploads to purchase everything. Hard currency was rarely utilized and stayed in banks for safekeeping. Lucky for us, the sturdy coins averted total destruction. "That's a lot of funds in a single month."

"These meccas were extremely successful. Delivery fees paid by the consumer were heavily taxed by the government. The companies profited excessively."

"Did workers earn a fair wage?" I asked, thinking back to a discussion I'd had with Darby about 3-D-printed homes and people who'd fled to rural areas but found no work. This location was certainly rural.

"Very few humans were employed. Meccas were fully automated. When maintenance bots became advanced enough to fix themselves, humans were no longer needed in any area of manufacturing. Wage amounts are unknown."

"Damn. What a mixed-up world," I said. "You could

get anything your heart desired within minutes, but affording those items had to be tough for a majority of the population."

"Creditors were abundant and were a requirement to keep the economy going," she replied. "The data suggests that, without them, the entire world would've financially imploded. The average human carried more than one million dollars in debt throughout their lifetime."

That was hard to believe. "My ancestors, it seems, were not easily satiated."

"Debt was accepted and normalized. Parents could assign debt to their offspring in utero to pay for their needs prior to birth."

"You're kidding me. I've never heard that before," I said, shocked. "So, by the time a child was of 'wage-earning' age, they already had a crushing amount of funds to repay?" That was a fairly depressing notion. Our ancestors had always been portrayed as greedy and lacking empathy in their pursuit of perfection. This information only validated that notion.

"That is correct. Wage-earning began at age eleven."

I thought back to the discarded bodies of the pregnant women we'd found when searching for the medi-pods. People had likely been forced to join whatever government program they could or starve. "If everyone could assume debt from birth, why were so many people poor?"

"Debt collection was structured and unyielding. If the consumer missed one payment after the age of twelve, his or her name was added to a restricted list. After subsequent default, that consumer was denied future credit, and any remaining funds were secured. With no credit, that person was unable to purchase anything. Physical currency was rarely traded in the mainstream world."

The flight recorder gave another small beep, and I banked Luce south. I was thankful the flight screen had stayed active after I unplugged Maisie. As an added bonus, the bottom right corner displayed a destination clock that flashed three hours and sixteen minutes. The time remaining to reach our target. "Currency wasn't traded by the mainstream populace, but it existed somewhere, or people without credit would've had nothing."

"Yes," she replied. "Physical currency was traded in the Outskirts. Items were limited, however, and their value inflated, oftentimes by a hundredfold. The Outskirts was a volatile place, and data shows humans were desperate, resorting to violence and thievery to survive."

"During one of our conversations, Lockland equated those places to war zones," I said thoughtfully. It was hard to believe that the world we occupied right now, with all its hardships and brutality, might be a more peaceful place to reside than in the Outskirts. "That term stuck. But we refer to outskirts now as people who live outside the city limits, not an area itself."

Maisie's lights flickered in rapid succession. "I detect a foreign craft thirty kilometers southwest. Its flight path indicates that it will not come within ten kilometers of our location."

I gripped the levers. I shouldn't be surprised there was a craft in the area, since people lived down here, but it was still unsettling. If the militia found out I was here, there would be no way to approach unnoticed. I'd be forced to turn back, which could result in Case's certain death, and making sure he lived to see another day was the current plan. "What kind of craft is it? Do you think its radar will detect us?" That would alert the pilot that another craft was in the area, and they might decide to investigate.

"From this distance, I cannot accurately assess the make and model of the dronecraft," she answered. "Standard operating radar detection for most crafts is five kilometers. More than that, and studies showed that the pilot would become distracted. Of course, enhancements for longer distances could be integrated at an additional cost."

"I guess we'll have to wait and see," I said. "Please scan continually for crafts and UACs from this point onward and search for anything on the ground that might be transmitting a signal. If we get discovered, the likelihood of Case surviving dips into an unacceptable range."

"I have enabled my stealth mode," she said. "Saving a human life requires optimal and continual processing."

"You have a stealth mode?" I asked. This did not disappoint.

"Yes, I have many modes," she replied. "Stealth

mode enhances all radar readings for tech and crafts."

"Well, that's good, then," I said, not knowing what else to say. Maisie had figured out the priority of this mission, from listening to our conversations, and she'd adjusted accordingly. "You continue to surprise me, but in a good way."

"It is not my preference to surprise you," Maisie replied. "Although, it is understandable. If Earth had not been involved in a cataclysmic event, my handler would have been well informed about my capabilities. You are not. This will result in miscommunication."

"It's too bad you didn't come with a training manual—"

"The incoming craft has changed trajectory," she interrupted. "Interception course is one-point-three kilometers, less than four minutes."

"*Shit,*" I sputtered as I killed the dash, effectively dismantling any radio waves Luce produced that the other craft could track. I was sorry to see Maisie's map disappear, unsure if it would come back on its own, but I'd deal with that later. "What are our choices to avoid physical detection?"

"Landing would be optimal but, given the time frame, not advisable. The only adequate option is—"

"Disappear into the clouds," I finished for her. "I know that's what you're going to say. But, honestly, I was hoping you had a better option in that egg-shaped brain of yours." I began our ascent into the vapor, my least-favorite spot to fly. Not to mention it was dark and I had to deactivate my running lights to avoid being spied by the passing craft. "Can you do me a favor and detect any solid matter in front of us well in advance of it tearing through the craft?" Iron particles were an issue, especially at two hundred and fifty kilometers an hour. Even the smallest stone could prove disastrous.

"Yes," she said. "I will maintain neutrino scanning for debris large enough to render us inoperable."

"Great." As the clouds enveloped Luce, I was surprised to see the area around us brighten. I assumed it was a radiant glow from a moon I'd never seen filtering through. "The clouds must be less concentrated here," I commented. "Or maybe the band of rocks and debris above us is thinner? Case told me there are areas down here where iron dust isn't as dense, which allows for electric charges to build up and cause pulse storms."

"Rocks and minerals, including iron, blanket the upper atmosphere," she said. "I am unable to access adequate data concerning mass, as it is continually shifting." With so much debris in the upper atmosphere, it would be suicide to breach the cloud layer, even though I'd been curious about what resided above our heads since I was a small child.

After about four minutes, I said, "Has the craft passed yet? It feels like we've been up here for an eternity."

"It is within three-point-seven kilometers. Time remaining for intercept is forty-seven seconds," she replied.

I held my breath, thankful the clouds were an option, even though my heart raced. It was unsettling not to be able to see anything. "When they fly by," I told her, "I want to know everything about the craft. How many people are inside, the make and model, and where you think they're headed."

"The W class, fourth production, contains two humans, both male. The electronics have been repaired, much like this craft, using parts from many others. Radar is working, but range is limited to three kilometers. Their current trajectory and velocity would put them in the city in less than one hour."

"*Damn*," I swore. The militia was already sending men up to the city. There was no way to warn my crew, but they would expect it, so that made me feel better. "Can you detect any weapons on board?"

"Scanning for weaponry," she said. "One Web laser, one full taser, and one Blaster found."

"Is that it?" I asked. "No bombs or hydro-grenades?"

"No hydrogen found. Other supplies include protein cakes, aminos, water, two thermal pads, additional clothing, macro-lenses, and three amplifiers."

"Sounds like they're going to engage in a little spying," I muttered. "I wish there was a way to inform Lockland and Bender."

"I detect a radio tower nearby," Maisie said. "Less than fifteen minutes away on our current path."

That wasn't a surprise. "Yeah, Reed said they had their own towers and bandwidths," I said. "It must've taken a long time to erect those."

"If I am within close range of a radio tower, I can transmit a message."

My gaze shot to the egg. "Are you serious?"

"Disaster Protocol automatically enabled radio communication capabilities in the event that wireless satellite communication ceased operation."

"Can you call them? Like a tech phone?" That might not be the best idea. "We don't want to alert the bad guys we have access to their bandwidths."

"I am operational as a tech phone," she said. "But I can also send a coded message."

"How?" I asked.

"Anything that generates a signal utilizes the same language. In the past, most household items were coded to process voice, text, and video for ease of use and to facilitate communication. Humans favored handheld devices, as well as video monitors and holograms, but standard items worked in a similar capacity. As of my last download, forty-six quadrillion communications occurred hourly throughout the world using these methods."

"You're talking about object-interfacing, aren't you?" I said. "I've found a few of those coded devices you're talking about over the years, but I've never had success in setting up a link between two. Honestly, why humans needed to communicate so often and through something like a lamp or a clock is beyond me."

"Yes, the formal name is object-interfacing," she said. "Humans enjoyed a vast amount of convenience. To get two objects to link, you would have to reconfigure them to use radio signals, if their programming included that fail-safe. Many did, but some did not."

"Is it safe for me to come out of the clouds now?" I asked.

"Yes," she replied. "The W4 craft is out of range. I detect no other crafts in the area."

I began the descent from the vapor. "I love the idea of sending a message, but as far as I know, my crew doesn't have a working interface nearby. I'm not sure how they'd receive your message."

"There are a few options," she said. "The strongest interface option is an unusual method of communication, but it would work."

"What's that?" I asked.

"The medi-pod."

Chapter 4

"The medi-pod is an object interface?" I asked. "Which one? The one in the government building? The one at the barracks? Or the one we uncovered at the facility out of town?" Maybe all of them were.

"The one powered by the fusion reactor," she answered. "The one the seeker Mary was put into."

"How did you know that? Are you always automatically scanning for that kind of stuff?" I was dumbfounded that Maisie knew things she hadn't revealed to us. But as she'd said before, her handler back in the day would've known her capabilities and what questions to ask. We were running blind.

"When the medi-pod was powered on, its software automatically searched for incoming radio waves and scanned my system. Its communication network is state of the art, allowing for remote programming, which functions like an object interface."

"That's incredible," I said. "So, how do you send a

message? Will it pop up on the readout screen?" Darby would see the communication if they were still using the medi-pod. I'd only left the building a short time ago, so the probability was high that Mary was still inside the medi-pod.

"Yes," she answered. "I will send a coded message that will render as text on the interface screen."

"Will he be able to reply?" I asked.

"I will include instructions for him to follow," she answered. "Darby's intelligence ranks in the ninety-seventh percentile for a human."

"How close to the radio tower do you need to be to link up?" I asked.

"To establish a connection, it's optimal to be within one kilometer. The medi-pod must accept my request to interface, and once it does, the bond will remain intact as long as I'm within range of a radio signal."

"What if the medi-pod doesn't accept your request?"

"It will," she said, her voice as steady and unwavering as ever. "Accepting it requires inputting an access code that was programmed by the software's authors, which is something I was designed to break."

"Good to know," I said. The only thing better than having a status reader was having an extremely confident status reader. "How close are we to the tower?"

"Six minutes," she answered. "It is safe to turn on your radio signal once again."

I flipped the switch on the dash. Thankfully, the flight recorder screen blinked back on, revealing the map Maisie had initiated. The trip time now read two hours and forty-three minutes.

"Direct the craft west twelve degrees," she instructed. "Continue for three minutes, then begin your descent. It is better if you land. The connection will take some time to establish."

I did as she asked.

It was darker out of the clouds. I turned my running lights back on. As I decreased altitude, a large, shiny shape revealed itself. Most radio towers in the city were made of rusted steel and wire, cobbled together on the tallest buildings left standing.

This one was entirely different.

It'd been built on a short hill devoid of any trees or life, and it had to be at least twenty to thirty meters high. It was tall and thin and constructed of either aluminum or titanium. I squinted at it through the windshield as Luce bounced once on her landing gear. "It looks like a ladder, but thick on the bottom, skinnier on top." I'd never seen anything like it. "Is that the way they're supposed to be constructed?"

"Yes," Maisie answered. "I will not be able to respond to your questions while initiating the interface."

"Okay," I said. "When you're done, I'm ready with the message." Darby would be surprised to receive it, but like Maisie said, he was smart enough to figure it out.

Instead of Maisie's lights flickering all over the place, she went dark.

I leaned forward. The craft was positioned at the base of the tower's short hill. The view below us, from what I could see in the low light, was dotted with a few dead trees and a couple of rocky outcroppings. Nothing more.

Drizzle pattered on the roof as I sat back. My mind drifted to Case. For the first time, I allowed myself to think about what happened to him. Since the discovery that he'd been taken, I'd remained in constant motion—returning to the government building, outlining a plan, packing, dealing with Mary—while convincing my crew that going after him was the right thing to do, which it was.

Now, my brain was filled with Case.

The outskirt had saved Daze over himself.

He'd selflessly made sure the kid was locked in the back room when the threat arrived. And knowing Case, he'd probably made a big ruckus to distract Tillman's men from doing anything but capturing him. I hadn't seen any bodies, nor had I noticed any blood, but the evidence had probably been there if I'd bothered to check.

Case had known that when he didn't arrive back at the government building, with Daze and Reed, at the allotted time, I would come after them. He had to have done something that made his captors exit the barracks immediately. Possibly telling them he had a bomb would've done the trick.

"Outskirt," I murmured under my breath, clasping my hands behind my head and tilting it up toward the sky. "Why didn't you just stall? I could've taken them out, and you'd still be here." Whether I actually would've been able to succeed was another story. But I certainly would've tried. If I'd been a few minutes earlier, I would have flown right into the middle of it. Expecting our secure location by the sea to be compromised hadn't entered my mind. If they'd been watching the skies, I would've been vulnerable.

Tillman and his men never would've found the barracks if Reed hadn't been injected with a tracker, which was infuriating. There were a lot of ways to track someone, but the fact Maisie hadn't detected it inside him meant it'd most likely been developed after her last download. Probably a bio-mimicking device, something that integrated with his body chemistry seamlessly. Daze had overheard one of the men say that Reed was too dumb to know he had a tracker on him. It could've been incorporated in something he ingested daily, such as his protein cakes.

I yanked off my helmet and set it on the floor of the passenger seat, rubbing my head with my hands. Wearing a helmet was second nature, but being without it felt good. I glanced down at Maisie, who was still dark.

Visualizing how I was going to break Case out of this bionics building wasn't an easy task. It would take ingenuity and help from Maisie to sneak past their security and implement a plan that had an adequate rate of success. If they had Babble, he would be getting a dose soon. If I were them, I would've made sure the outskirt stayed unconscious the entire trip. Or he would be a handful.

A jolt of anxiety wound its way through my body.

I hoped they hadn't harmed him too badly. Case was as hard as they came, but everyone had their limits.

Getting a message to my crew would be invaluable. I was more than a little in awe of Maisie and her abilities. Rescuing Case would have been a lot trickier—bordering on impossible—without the status reader, which was why Lockland had insisted on a projected sixty percent success rate.

Maisie's lights blinked twice before arcing slowly around the craft. "The connection is complete," she intoned. "The interface has been established."

"Fantastic," I replied with genuine excitement, stopping just short of clapping my hands together. "Here's the message I want you to send: Darby, it's Holly. Maisie found a way to access the medi-pod as an interface. The militia just sent two men your way, likely to keep watch and report back. I'll reach my destination in about two hours. Maisie is sending instructions on how to communicate with us. I'll keep you posted."

Maisie was quiet for a few moments before she said, "Message delivered."

Well, that had been painless. "How long do you think it's going to take Darby to answer?" I started Luce, her props winding up as I eased her off the ground.

"Formulating a reply will require Darby to integrate the pico with the medi-pod operating system," she said. "It should take him no longer than thirty minutes."

I knew Darby could handle it. "Will you be able to receive the message while we're flying?"

"Yes, as long as I'm within range of the selected bandwidth," she replied. "I detect another tower fifty kilometers south. By extrapolating that information with the location of this tower, I can say that there is a high likelihood there will be others within similar distances along the way."

"That's a fair assumption. They need those towers to communicate," I said. "Once we get near the target, we have to determine where to land well outside the range of their monitoring system. I'm certain they keep a close eye on the perimeter. When we accidentally flew above their airspace before, by the time we spotted the building, they'd already launched a craft after us. I'm not sure how much distance to estimate, or whether they track by radar, visual, or both, but we're going to have to decide a safe distance to set down ahead of time." It was a little worrisome, because if they were monitoring twenty to thirty kilometers out, I'd have to find a way in on foot, which would take a full day or more, and Case didn't have that much time to spare.

"I may be able to interrupt their feed," Maisie said. "I won't know if that is plausible until I detect what they are using."

"That would be amazing," I said. The Maisie miracles kept coming. "Should I stop at the next tower?"

"Yes," she said. "That is advisable. With a strong radio connection, I may be able to discover their system at a greater distance."

"Will do," I said. We would reach it within ten minutes.

We rode in silence, my thoughts returning to Case. The outskirt had better stay alive. I knew what he had endured his entire life, so it was more than a little heartbreaking to think of him being subjected to more torture. But the man was tough—tough enough to survive on his own as a child. He'd find a way to hang on.

After a bit, Maisie said, "Tower detected ten kilometers south by southeast."

I was watching for it, but hadn't seen anything yet. I banked Luce in that direction and began our descent. A few minutes later, I had visual. This radio tower looked like an exact replica of the last one. It sat on a short hill, nothing else around it, and had been erected in a ladderlike configuration, larger at the bottom, skinnier at the top.

Maisie went dark as I set Luce down.

I let her do her thing, hoping she'd be able to figure out something about the militia base that would help us get in closer.

"Completing scan of their system," Maisie said. After a moment, she confirmed, "Results uncertain."

"Damn," I said. "Well, it was worth a try."

"I detect another tower sixty-two kilometers southwest," she said. "Using this information to calculate, there will be a minimum of five towers between here and our destination."

"So, we stop at each one until you can tap into their system?" I asked, starting Luce. It was going to cost us time, but it would be worth it, especially if Maisie could get us in under the radar.

"That is correct." As I launched Luce into the air, Maisie's lights gave two distinct pulses. A second later, she said, "Receiving incoming message."

"From Darby?" I asked eagerly.

Instead of answering my dumb question—because who else would she be getting a message from?—she recited the missive, surprising me by using Darby's own voice, sampled from her database. "Holy crap, Holly. I had no idea sending a message like this was even possible. I relayed the information to Lockland and Bender. Lockland wants you to try to get us word once an hour, if possible. Good luck."

"Maisie, send this message back," I instructed. "I'll send updates as often as I can. Maisie believes she might be able to infiltrate the militia's radar system, allowing us to fly in undetected. How's Mary?"

It took Darby a full minute to respond. When he did, Maisie recited, still modulating in his voice, "She just exited the pod. She's doing well. She says thank you again."

"Awesome," I said. "I'll talk to you soon."

"Take care, Holly," Maisie replied, this time a little quicker. "Bender says, 'Stay alive or else.'"

I chuckled, shaking my head at the miracle that was the status reader. "Maisie, you're full of surprises. That sounded exactly like Darby."

"Voice modulation requires only a small sample to be effective."

"Glad to hear it," I said. "I'm sure that will come in handy on more than one occasion."

Chapter 5

Luce was perched at the base of the fifth radio tower. We were less than forty minutes outside of the militia's headquarters. If Maisie couldn't get through this time, we were going to have to risk moving closer without knowing how far the militia's surveillance extended.

I waited—not so patiently—for Maisie to connect to their system, trying to fortify myself for another disappointment, when Maisie blinked twice and said, "Link established."

Sitting up, I gasped. "You got through? Can you shut down their radar so we can get in unseen?"

"Negative," she answered. I slumped back in my seat. That wasn't the news I'd hoped for. "A complete shutdown is impossible. Their power grid is secured with an adequate backup."

"I suppose I shouldn't be surprised," I said. "They've had years to perfect their system."

"While a shutdown is not an option," Maisie continued, "scrambling their feed for the time needed to breach their perimeter appears to be an acceptable substitution."

I sat up again, my heart beginning to race.

We'd been in the air for almost two hours, stopping dutifully at every tower along the way with no results. "Scrambling will absolutely work." If Maisie could interrupt their feed long enough for me to fly through undetected, it would be the same as shutting their radar down. We just had to make sure we weren't visually spotted along the way.

"Detecting distance radar capabilities," she said. After a moment, she relayed, "They are scanning thirty-five kilometers in every direction."

"That's not as far as I thought," I said, peering at my dash. "We can't afford any mistakes, so we land inside fifty kilometers, you do your scrambling, and I'll get us in and situated as quickly as possible."

"There is another tower one hundred kilometers from here," she said. "That will place us sixty-three-point-seven kilometers from our destination, twenty-eight-point-seven kilometers outside of their range."

"Perfect," I said, punching Luce on. "From that distance, will you be able to detect humans?"

"No," she replied. "My range for accurate bio detection is fifteen kilometers."

"How about other structures and places to hide a craft?"

"For a precise reading of the area, once again, fifteen kilometers is essential."

"Can you scramble their radar and perform both tasks at the same time?"

"No," she answered. "Interrupting their bandwidth will consume my capacity."

Damn. That was going to make this harder.

Not impossible, just more difficult.

I had an idea. "Can you analyze the buildings in the area, specifically the ones that used to stand near our target, and give me an estimate on which ones you think might still be intact? I didn't notice any other structures beneath us the first time we flew over, but I was distracted." Case grabbing the controls and effectively pushing us into the clouds during a pulse storm had diverted my attention.

"Assessing engineering data of nearby structures," she said. Fairly quickly, she followed with, "Architectural design for Robo Limb shows the building was constructed in concrete forms, a relatively outdated technology used only when threat of on-site explosion exceeded fifty percent. Other structures in the area have a less than two percent chance of having retained their structure."

"Interesting," I said. "The manufacturing of their robotic appendages must've involved some sort of chemical reaction." The government safeguarded against things like that. "That aged construction technique may have saved the building. Concrete forms are heavy-duty. Check and see if anything else in the area utilized those same materials." I pushed Luce to her limits, nearing two hundred and seventy-five kilometers per hour. I was anxious to get on the ground and get Case the hell out of there.

"Most of the other buildings within this mecca were constructed of a typical interlaced steel and graphene framing. The only similar type of construction were the mag-lev tunnels. A few of the buildings did have concrete foundation systems, but they were not constructed with concrete above ground level."

My interest piqued.

Given that some of the tunnels in the city had held up when battered by the aftereffects of the meteor, there was a chance these tunnels had also survived. "That might be exactly what we need. How far are they from the militia headquarters?"

"They are two-point-four kilometers from our destination."

"Is there any standing water in the area?" I asked. Flooded tunnels would be a different story.

"I am too far away to detect environmental factors. But other than a drainage system throughout the mecca," Maisie answered, "this location is dry. It was chosen for its flat, uninterrupted expanse. A containment unit was erected to provide water to the area, but it's unknown if it is still standing."

"Perfect," I said. "I'll head for the nearest tunnel, then. I should be able to find a way in, assuming the mag-lev trains weren't dug too deeply underground."

"Some of the industrial trains operated in tubes above ground, some below, depending on the topography. The six mag-levs docked at this mecca were below ground."

"So, I head to the center, where all the trains converged. Then pick a tunnel that looks clear?"

"Theoretically, that is correct," she replied. "It is unknown if the trains were at the station at the time of impact. The chances are unlikely that all six were there. There will be no way to tell until we get within visual proximity."

"Six gives me nice odds. I'll take it," I said, one eye on the flight recorder to monitor the time. I'd need to set down shortly. "Having you busy scrambling the radar when we enter the area heightens our risk of detection, but if I have a set destination, I believe I can do it."

"To increase the likelihood of success, plug my lifecable back into the flight recorder," she instructed. "I will provide the coordinates for the train station, along with a path that will be out of visual detection from inhabitants within the headquarters." I did as she asked, watching the screen blink and change as new information was uploaded. When she was done, she announced, "Destination logged."

I disconnected her and set her back down. "The next tower should be coming up soon," I said.

"Yes," she replied. "Arrival in seven minutes."

We flew in silence, then I decided to ask Maisie, "Are you programmed to worry?" I was curious if her software had any ability to mimic human emotions. "Is something like that part of your makeup?"

"No. I am not programmed to worry," she answered. "Experiencing human emotion is not part of my design. However, I am able to detect and diagnose human physical and emotional states, so I can better interpret and respond to the world around me."

"What are you picking up from me now?" I asked.

"Rapid breathing. Disrupted speech patterns. Concentrated perspiration," she answered. "With this data, I calculate your worry factor to be greater than five on a ten-point scale."

"What about fear?" I asked. "Can you calculate fear on the same scale?"

"Fear is measured by quaking cadence, spiked pulse rates, and scent."

"You have a sense of *smell*?" Gasping at Maisie's admissions was now becoming the norm.

"I have several small perforations located on the exterior of my shell that allow my system to analyze air molecules. A fearful human releases a stress hormone from the adrenal gland called cortisol. My sensors are equipped to detect this hormone."

"Wow," I said. "That's incredible. They thought of everything when they made you."

"Yes. I am equipped for many scenarios. Assessing the mental and physical well-being of soldiers in my charge is essential."

"You're specialized for combat?" I asked. Even though she was a military-grade status reader, I'd assumed she was designed as an intelligence operative, or something close.

"Yes. My primary designation was to accompany troops into the field."

I glanced down at the egg, raising an eyebrow. "Did you ever go on a mission?"

"No," she replied. "I was not activated until after Lockland found me."

"Are you disappointed?"

"I do not feel disappointment. However, our current combat mission closely correlates with the prime directives in my operating system."

"It's true, we're on a mission." I chuckled. "But I'm no soldier."

"According to my database, a soldier is defined as a person who is faithfully enlisted to serve and defend a populace and its freedoms. I believe, Holly, you are the definition of a soldier." Her lights flickered. "The radio tower is two-point-four kilometers southwest."

I eased back on the propulsion as the tower and its reflective materials twinkled into view. It was just as shiny as the others. Once we were on the ground, I told her, "Do your thing. When Luce breaches their perimeter, I'll be able to push her close to three hundred kilometers per hour. That means I'll need you to scramble their signals for approximately ten minutes so I can reach the tunnels undetected."

"There is another radio tower in close range," she said after a few minutes. "This will allow me to triangulate the signal. I will initiate interference at the forty-kilometer mark. Each minute in the air diminishes our success rate by six-point-three percentage points."

"Are you telling me I'll need to go faster than three hundred?" I asked. "I'm not sure I can do that. Luce begins to shake like she's about to break up around two ninety."

"This craft is built to handle a large stress load. The motors are updated and balanced. By my calculations, three hundred and seventy-four kilometers per hour will exert maximum allowable compression on all parts. But this speed cannot be sustained for more than twelve minutes without risk of full system amperage failure and physical harm to outer panels."

I whistled. "Three hundred and seventy-four? Are you sure? I've never stressed her that far. Maybe we should boost instead?" A hydro-boost lasted only a few minutes, but any stress was taken off the system, since it bypassed the motors completely.

"Max speed will be sufficient," Maisie answered. "Using the hydro-boost upon retreat will increase the odds of escaping unharmed."

"You have a point there." I bit my lip. "Okay, I'm ready if you are."

"My connection points have been established," she said. "Proceed to target destination. Once inside the surveillance zone, I will alert you, then I must go dark."

"Is that your way of telling me I'll be on my own?" I said as I took us into the air. "Believe it or not, I've survived this long without a status reader by my side and have managed to keep breathing. I'm pretty sure I can do it again for six minutes."

"The odds of your survival are enhanced by my knowledge," she helpfully pointed out.

"That's correct," I agreed. "I wouldn't even attempt this mission without you." I likely would, otherwise Case would die. But it would've gone an entirely different way—the way of my luck running out.

"Your projected rate of success without me, which includes a significant increase in severe bodily damage and likely death, are below sixty percent," she said.

"You overheard Lockland's instructions to me, I take it," I said. "In calculating that rate, did you account for my awesome combat skills? Or are you ranking me based on the average soldier in your database?"

"An average soldier would not attempt this solo mission," she replied. "He or she would be ill-equipped to encounter the perils you will be facing. By my analysis, this mission under normal circumstances would require at least six soldiers to complete."

"With six, are the odds guaranteed?" I asked.

"No," she said.

"How do you rank my personal ability to get the job done?" I had no idea if she could calculate such a thing, but she'd let me know if she couldn't.

"Ninety-three-point-nine percent."

I raised an eyebrow. "That's pretty generous. Why so high? Especially when you just told me I was significantly more likely to be grievously injured or killed without your help."

"Your tenacity and assuredness, coupled with fearlessness and aggression, give you a quantifiable advantage."

"That sounds like a human calculation."

"My system compiles strategic accuracies based on facts, as well as the human condition. According to my data, there are frequent instances in which an individual should have failed, but succeeded due to one deciding factor."

"What's that?" I asked as I sped Luce toward our destination. "Fearlessness or aggression?"

"Love."

Chapter 6

"I'm not in *love* with Case," I sputtered. "That's just…just…"

"Your verbal hesitation indicates uncertainty."

"Oh, I'm certain all right. I might admit to a growing fondness for him. After all, he did just save the kid. But that's not *love.* The outskirt causes me nothing but headaches and trouble."

"Your vitals contradict your response. Your heart rate has spiked. Your increasing chest respirations indicate—"

"It's not love. End of discussion."

"Your response is confusing. When you are around him, your physical reaction becomes—"

"It's not confusing," I insisted, cutting her off. "I'm stating a fact. Drop it." I couldn't believe an inanimate object was accusing me of being in love with Case. That was beyond ridiculous.

"Beginning radar disruption now," Maisie announced, thankfully changing the topic.

That was my cue to push Luce to her absolute maximum.

I engaged the propulsion, coaxing my craft to go

faster than I ever had before. Maisie had assured me that I could keep my dashboard operable until my target was in sight, which was a requirement for getting the job done. Without it, I wouldn't be able to clock distance or see the destination marker on the flight screen.

At this speed, I'd reach the convergence of the mag-lev tunnels in just under seven minutes.

Following the directions, I banked north, taking a wide berth around the building to avoid visual detection. The sun would be rising soon, but the cloak of darkness was still on our side. As I neared, I switched off my running lights. No need to act like a beacon.

Three minutes into the flight, Maisie's lights began to dance around, bouncing off the ceiling and windshield.

That wasn't a good sign. I glanced over, concerned. "Are you still engaged?" I asked, not knowing if she would answer.

"They have...detected...my interference," she stuttered, her normally modulated voice sounding fractured.

"I'll be there in less than three minutes."

Her lights continued to blink. I pointed the craft due south, making a turn that felt sharper at this speed.

"They are initiating...a new system," she said. "Once engaged, it will...obliterate my ability to—"

"Landing in one minute, thirty-eight seconds. Try to hold on." Outside the windshield, a patch of ground came into view. It was in shambles, rocks and boulders strewn everywhere. Part of a train lay on its side.

At least I knew we were in the right place.

Even if their radar came online now, we should still avoid detection. I powered off my radio communications, now that I had visual confirmation on the target, effectively shutting everything down.

We were so close to pulling this off.

Maisie's lights began to pulse as I headed in for a landing, not knowing where exactly I was going until I saw it. A tunnel opening to the left looked about Luce's size and was unobstructed. I angled her in, shutting down the props a meter above the ground. I was gliding in blind, hoping for the best.

We got lucky.

The space inside was clear enough to land. A few large rocks made the ground uneven, but it worked. I yanked back on the right lever twice as hard as usual to compensate for the lack of power and set her down.

Once we were settled, I leaned back in my seat, my head on the headrest, my breathing evening out. "Did we escape their detection?" I asked.

It took her a few seconds to reply. "Yes. They enacted another scanning system, but it was too late."

Relief flooded me. "Do they suspect someone has entered the area?"

"It is unclear how they will view my interference," she said. "They reacted swiftly when I jammed the signal, which indicates they had a protocol to follow and enabled it speedily."

"If they have a backup system, failure might be a frequent problem. If that's true, then they won't suspect anything yet. Can you tap into their bandwidths so we can keep track of their communications?"

"Yes," she said. "At this time, there is no activity, which would indicate that everyone is currently located inside the headquarters."

"Can you scan the building from here?" I asked.

"At two kilometers, I can receive a general human bio-reading," she answered. "But individualized stats and identification need to be taken within a sixty-meter range."

"How many humans are inside?"

As her lights did their thing, tossing out NeuDAR and lidar into the ether, I grabbed a pack filled with essentials from the backseat and strapped it on, opening my door, which scraped along the ground. I swore.

She replied, "I detect one hundred and eighty-four humans in the area, all of them inside."

I stepped out onto the rocky ground, my Gem aloft, ducking back into the craft to get Maisie, cupping her in my palm. Rain lightly fell outside the tunnel as the day began to dawn, visibility brightening by the minute. I hated that we were going to have to do this during daylight hours, but Case needed us now.

There was a good chance that the militia would send out scouts to make sure no one had infiltrated the area when their system blipped. "I'm sticking you in my pocket so you can stay protected," I told her as I opened my vest and placed her near my heart. "I'm going to need you to scan continually for humans and crafts in the immediate vicinity. Alert me if you detect anything. Which direction should I head?" I exited the tunnel at a low crouch, examining my surroundings. It was still too dark to gauge anything accurately, but this was definitely the confluence of the mag-lev tunnels. Not only were there six large tunnel openings, but there were several paved roads crisscrossing them, where I assumed delivery trucks and drones would've landed to facilitate moving goods in and out. According to Maisie, this mecca had been a big business, earning trillions in revenue. It would've been essential to get merchandise in and out as quickly as possible. The tunnels were much bigger than the ones in the city, indicating that the trains were larger than those that transported people. From what I'd read, the interiors contained very few seats. Space was reserved for product only.

Maisie's voice was slightly muffled as she answered, "Proceed southeast toward your destination. No humans or operational crafts detected."

Turning, I crawled up a short embankment outside the tunnel. The height gave me a view of the area, which was desolate. Debris was scattered everywhere, but it was hard to say where it'd come from, as there were no distinct outlines marking other buildings or structures in the vicinity.

I began to jog, my Gem out front, my gaze scanning the landscape in a grid formation, making sure I missed nothing. I dropped my visor to check infrared, just to be sure.

No heat signatures that I could detect.

"In one kilometer," I told Maisie, "I want you to assess which way gives us the most cover. If they send scouts, we need to be able to keep out of sight. The last few meters are going to be the trickiest." That wasn't counting breaching the building and getting a possibly injured Case free. After almost a kilometer, I slowed, ducking behind a partial wall left over from a small, unidentifiable structure. "I need that route now."

"Continue on your current path for sixty-seven meters, then veer right for one hundred and forty. I detect several inoperable crafts, maintenance tools, and a structure with a roof. No human bio signatures."

"Okay, once we get there, how close will we be to our target?"

"You will be within sight of it," she answered.

I began to jog. "Alert me when I need to change direction."

After the allotted time, Maisie announced, "Turn right."

As soon as I made the turn, I spotted the structure she was talking about. "Looks like a maintenance shack," I murmured. I was almost there when Maisie made a beeping noise I'd never heard before.

"Warning, warning," she stated. "I detect movement outside the headquarters. Two unidentified males are approaching in a single craft, and two unidentified males are heading this way on foot. If they continue on their current trajectory, they will intercept us in four-point-three minutes."

Rather than go into the maintenance structure, which wasn't really a contained building, as it had only three walls, one side completely open, I ducked behind it, managing to shield myself from detection before the men arrived.

Once there, I ran the length of the building, poking my head out the other side, immediately catching sight of the headquarters in the distance. It was no more than a hundred meters away. I watched as two men got into a craft parked outside and took off, thankfully in the opposite direction.

We had arrived at our destination.

"We have to stay here until the two men approaching leave," I whispered to Maisie, settling my shoulder against a patch of corrugated steel, the overhang keeping us out of the rain for the moment. "Don't make a sound. If you have to speak, do it at the lowest decibel for human hearing." Maisie did me proud by not answering.

After a moment, I made my way back to the middle of the structure where I'd seen some gaps in the corrugation. I crouched down, peering through as the men entered from the other side.

"I don't know why they have us out here so early." A tall man dressed in a dark jumpsuit addressed a shorter man wearing synthetic leather pants and a jacket. "There's no way anybody's getting into this area without us knowing."

Yeah, about that.

"It's because the guys from the city are here," the shorter guy retorted. "They're paranoid. Travis said something about our radar flipping out for a couple minutes. But that shit happens all the time. They got it up and running in no time. I don't know what they're so worried about."

"They brought a prisoner back," the guy in the jumpsuit said as he headed toward a table scattered with tools. I edged a few centimeters closer, wishing I'd had time to set up an amplifier before they arrived. "I haven't seen the poor bastard, but I heard he's in rough shape."

Case was alive. I'd take *in rough shape* over *dead.*

The guy in synthetic leather walked over to one of the crafts that Maisie had mentioned and hoisted the pilot door. The jumpsuit guy followed, picking a few tools off the table and opening the craft's motor cover. "He's part of that group they're worried about," he said as he sat in the pilot seat. I had to strain to hear him. "They're trying to get him to talk, but he's being obstinate as hell."

Way to go, Case.

"Tillman just sent a couple guys back to their base to get Babble," the jumpsuit guy said as he began to tinker with the motor. "He'll talk soon enough." Then the man swore, flinging one of his tools to the ground with a clatter and shaking his hand rapidly. "Dammit. There's no way we're getting this craft running, especially not within a day. Hysteria is not good for anyone."

Hysteria, huh?

The guy in synthetic leather emerged from the craft and walked around to the front to take a look, hands on his hips. "We don't have enough crafts to evacuate everyone anyway."

"Exactly," the other guy replied. "One more isn't going to help. What are they so worried about anyway? I didn't even have time to eat my breakfast."

"They're worried about shit raining down on us before the takeover is complete."

"Yeah, like it's ever going to happen," the jumpsuit guy muttered. "They've been talking about this since I was a kid. Never going to work."

So the group had skeptics. Interesting.

We'd discovered that this militia held strong, long-indoctrinated beliefs. The group was established after a man named Brock Shannon killed seekers when his wife became infected with Plush. They believed if they cleansed the city of unworthy humans, The Water Initiative would come back, and everything would suddenly be happy and healthy again. Or something like that. It was hard to know exactly.

The guy in synthetic leather slapped a hand against the other guy's chest, rocking him backward. "You can't say stuff like that out loud, Jones. They'll have you in Shannon's Chair before lunchtime. Especially in this climate. Ever since that craft flew above us a week ago, they've been on edge. Now these guys are down from the city, and they won't tell us what's going on. It's better if we just put our heads down and fix this thing."

The craft that had passed over them was Seven, and I'd been piloting her. I had no idea what the Shannon Chair was, but it sounded like they used it to penalize, or reindoctrinate, people. Both options sounded grim.

Jones, the jumpsuit guy, went over to pick up the tool he'd flung away, his hand obviously feeling better. "I don't know why they can't program the LiveBots to do this crap. How are we supposed to know how to put these pieces back together? We don't even have the right parts."

LiveBots?

The guy in synthetic leather headed to a stool and sat, chuckling. "Those bots were programmed to sell luxury items, not fix crafts."

"The world as our ancestors know it ends, and instead of finding a warehouse full of mechanic bots, we get lousy retail bots."

"Hey, it could've been worse," the guy on the stool retorted. "We could've gotten gardening bots or self-care bots. At least these ones are nice to look at."

They had working LiveBots.

Chapter 7

LiveBots changed everything.

I needed to get to a safe place where I could consult with Maisie. Working robots—who knew how many?—affected my approach and projected success rate. The dynamic had shifted completely with this news. A LiveBot working security couldn't be disabled as quickly as a human. It would take a lot of firepower, hitting it in the exact right place, to bring one down. I wasn't even sure, since I'd never fought one before. In the meantime, his pals would have a clear shot at me. The militia could essentially defeat me without a single man lifting a weapon.

I turned to retreat, not sure where to go, when Maisie's voice came through extremely quietly. I stopped, plucking her out of my pocket and settling her against my ear. "Repeat," I whispered, making my way down to the end, where I'd have a visual of the headquarters.

"A message has come through from Darby," she said, her voice barely audible.

"Tell him I can't talk right now," I said under my breath. "Also, tell him that the militia has LiveBots, and I'll be in touch as soon as I can."

Keeping Maisie in my hand, I ducked my head around, peeking at the building I planned to infiltrate. Little bits of cover stood between it and me—a boulder here, a dead tree there. Not enough to keep me well concealed for any length of time. "Maisie, I'm going to need you to assess the exact number of LiveBots inside. Can you do that?"

"Scanning initiated," she replied. "I detect twenty-three AI-compatible LiveBots."

"And just to clarify, that's in addition to the hundred and eighty-four humans you detected earlier?" I asked.

"Yes," she answered.

"Crap," I muttered. "They can station all twenty-three between me and them and not risk a single human life on their end. There's no way I can successfully repel or disarm that many robots. You have to blow up both their cerebral circuit board and their data receptors. If you don't, they can still function." Or so I'd heard. The only LiveBot I'd ever encountered was Trina down South. And she had hardly been in any kind of working condition.

"That is correct," Maisie answered. "LiveBots were designed to withstand attacks by humans."

I glanced around, not seeing much else on the

barren landscape. "Where did the LiveBots come from?" My lips were only a few centimeters from Maisie's shell. "Those guys said they were retail bots."

"Accessing history of the area," she said as I transferred her back to the shell of my ear, straining to hear. "This mecca contained a manufacturing facility that specialized in LiveBots programmed to sell luxury items. The retail bots were installed in stores in major cities around the world."

"I'm not familiar with how specialized LiveBots worked," I said. "If they were made solely for retail, are they only programmed to do that specific job?"

"Yes," Maisie answered. "Their software is limited, focused on the selling of merchandise and nothing more."

"Are they capable of carrying out security duties?"

"They would be programmed to perform light security—for example, deterring shoplifters. But they would not be programmed to carry or use a weapon."

"Do they have a freedom option like you do? One that we could enable?" I asked, hope at the forefront. If Maisie could set them free, she could have some control over them.

"No," she said. "Their AI compatibility for freedom is nonexistent. However, if their database has the ability to accept uploads, to facilitate a transfer or purchase by another company, it might be possible to insert a parallel program containing additional language to expand their usefulness."

"Is that something you could do?" I asked.

"Not on my own," she answered. "The program must be written externally. Once it's complete, I would be able to upload the data. But success would be limited if their firewall is activated."

"What's a firewall?" I asked, glancing over my shoulder. If the men heard me conversing out here, my cover would be blown. I had to exit this area quickly, but I wasn't sure where to go. I brought Maisie back up to my ear as she began to answer.

"A firewall protects a bot's system. It limits or blocks programs from uploading or downloading," she said. "Some firewalls are temporary, and some are permanent. If the feature is permanent, once a LiveBot has fulfilled its duties, it is discarded. If the firewall is temporary, it can be adapted for new work."

"Why would any manufacturer make a firewall permanent? What's the point in building a robot at great expense, then throwing it in the trash instead of refurbishing it?" I was confused, which was increasing the level of my voice. I had to be careful.

"If a firewall wasn't permanent, it was vulnerable to hackers," she answered. "According to my records, most firewalls for retail bots, once activated, were permanent. Owners were not willing to risk having their merchandise stolen. If a hacker gained control of their program, the bot could simply walk out of a store with the goods."

"Damn hackers," I grumbled. "Still causing trouble. Can you detect if the firewall is engaged?"

"Yes," she answered. "But it will take time. I must scan each system individually."

"Okay, do that. We have no other choice," I said. "Once you're finished, I want an update and location on Case. While you're busy, I'll find a safe place for us to take cover." I spotted a small boulder approximately fifteen meters away, out of sight of the militia headquarters. Before I could make my move, props sounded in the distance. A craft was entering the area, and by the sound of the incoming noise, it was headed toward us. I had no choice but to stay under the overhang, keeping out of sight from the air. I made my way back toward the middle, crouching by the small gap to hear what the men were saying.

"That must be the scouts coming back," the guy in synthetic leather said as he walked out to the front of the building.

Jones retorted, "I heard they found Cannon up north. Or what was left of him. He was shot through the neck at the building they were staking out. They haven't found Abel, but they think he might've been blown up."

"That's what they get for trusting a guy like Reed," the leather guy complained. "I don't care if his father was one of the original founders, he's cocky, arrogant, and stupid as shit."

Yes, he was.

We'd known Reed's father was important, since he'd mentioned him when he was under the influence of Babble, but it was new information that his father was one of the founders. Reed had also told us his father was dead.

The craft landed in front of the two guys. Once the props powered down, both doors opened. "Find anything?" Jones called as he moved forward.

I couldn't hear the response because they were too far away. Instead, I sat back, resting my head against the steel. "This place is bustling with activity," I muttered. "How are we supposed to get in unseen?"

Maisie's lights poked through the spaces between my fingers. I brought her to my ear. She murmured, "Possible breach detected. Out of the nineteen LiveBots I scanned, two have severely damaged firewall systems."

I stood, transitioning her to my lips. "Great news," I whispered excitedly, making sure my voice was no louder than a breath. "Now you have to explain what that means."

"It means I have an opportunity to redirect those two LiveBots' command centers."

"And if we can do that," I said, "we can make them do our bidding?"

"Theoretically."

I pressed her firmly against my ear, straining to hear her over the rumblings of the men on the other side of the steel.

"Upon initial setup," she said, "the owner initiates primary voice-activated imprints. The robot is then programmed to follow only the primary's commands, or those the primary specifies. That way, unauthorized humans have no control over the LiveBot in public settings. I won't know until I access their software, but it seems these two have been activated previously, and there has been significant interference. The militia may have tried to override the primary commands, thus damaging the firewall. But the bots appear to be in working order, so whatever action was taken didn't disarm them completely."

"Sounds complex," I murmured. "How quickly do you think you can reroute them?"

"It will take at least thirty minutes to access their internal systems," she said. "But, to take on such a task, proximity is important. I must be closer to achieve full integration."

"How close are you talking?" I asked, dread creeping in.

"Directly outside the building," she answered.

My heart thumped loudly in my chest.

"This task is complicated," she said. "Trying to achieve the same result from this distance would take hours."

"Okay," I said. "But getting there is going to be tough. There's barely any cover, and blackout is over. People are buzzing around the sky, and according to the two men inside the structure, the folks in the headquarters are being extra cautious. They recognize that your interference might mean there's a problem." The outskirt was in that building right now—in rough shape, according to Jones and his buddy—and we needed to get him out. "Please scan for Case. I want to know his vitals."

It didn't take her long. "I have located Case. He is below ground. Vitals stable. Multiple contusions and skin abrasions detected. One minor fracture in the trapezoid. Costal cartilage separated from rib bone on left side. Chest respirations steady, but labored. Arms and legs secured by steel cuffs."

"So, you're telling me he's okay?" I asked with an eagerness I couldn't disguise. That didn't mean I *loved* him. It meant I was happy he wasn't dead. That was all.

"His injuries are not life-threatening at this time, but seeking medical attention is advisable."

"Of course. We're getting him into a medi-pod as soon as possible." I pondered what to do. We couldn't sit outside this structure for much longer. But heading to the boulder for cover would expose us to crafts from above. "Maisie, we have to find a way to get closer. Any ideas?"

"Detailing the area," she said.

Before she could respond, a loud noise came from inside the building. Something had clattered to the ground. A man shouted, "I don't care! Go out back and empty that fucking thing before it burns a hole in someone."

Out back was where I was.

Time to move.

I headed straight for the rock, since there was no other cover in sight. I slid behind it, landing on my backside, careful not to jam my pack against the hard surface. I had bombs inside, after all.

Footsteps rounded the maintenance shack a few moments later. "What an asshole," the guy muttered, sloshing something onto the ground. "This stuff only burns if it's concentrated. As it is, it's watered down. It wouldn't hurt an infant, much less a grown man."

I didn't know what he was talking about and didn't care.

As long as my location wasn't compromised, everything remained fine. My head stayed bent as I assessed the expanse in front of me.

Maisie's voice was low. I lifted her to my ear. "I detect a small drainage ditch thirty-seven meters southeast. Its position winds you near the target. It is deep enough to keep you concealed."

"Wonderful," I whispered. "But how am I supposed to jog thirty-seven meters and not be seen?"

"Humans in the area are distracted," she replied. "The percentage of success, without detection, is seventy-nine percent."

"Seventy-nine, huh? Those are better odds than the agreed-upon sixty."

"I will alert you if any of the humans change position."

"That's comforting," I started, "but by the time you warn me, I'll be in midrun with no cover. I either make it or I don't. If we're detected, it changes everything."

The man had walked back around the structure. I didn't hear anyone else moving around.

It was now or never.

I took off, keeping Maisie to my ear. "Direct me southeast."

"Head to the right two meters," she instructed. "Continue on this path—"

"I see it." I tucked her back into my pocket, my legs bent, Gem out.

When I arrived at the embankment, I leaped over the edge.

Chapter 8

I landed in cold, thigh-high, rusty water. After the initial shock, I slogged my way through the drainage ditch, finally making it to my destination. The building was in sight.

I was soaking wet, stinky, and almost completely frozen.

My taser was out of commission, but my HydroSol should work, even though it was waterlogged. My Gem had stayed lofted in the air, so it'd been protected from damage upon entry, but just barely. Not many weapons worked when they were wet. My pack had kept fairly dry, and I'd been lucky that my entry into the stagnant pool of rainwater—and who knew what else—hadn't jarred the contents inside too much. If it had, I wouldn't be here.

Peeking over the embankment, I surveyed the area. The back of the building was approximately twenty meters from where I crouched. "Any news?" I whispered to Maisie.

The status reader had engaged the first LiveBot when she'd deemed us close enough. I'd been at least fifteen minutes.

She didn't answer, which I took as a good sign.

I was antsy to get out of this cesspool and feel my toes again, but I didn't dare crawl out now and risk being exposed. I'd positioned myself at the corner of the building for a good reason. The angle of the windows, which contained real glass, would make it difficult to detect my location. I weighed my options. If Maisie was successful, we wouldn't have to wait until blackout. If she wasn't, darkness would give me the cover I needed, but freezing to death in this ditch was a concern and so was getting Case out in a timely fashion.

Maisie murmured something from my pocket that I couldn't hear. I drew her out and whispered into her shell, "You have permission to speak a little louder. Are you in control of the LiveBot?"

"No," she answered, modulating her voice appropriately. "But I am inside her program. Accessing her response controls now." Patience had never been one of my virtues, and that held true now. Before I could pester Maisie to work faster, she said, "I have successfully penetrated her firewall. Not only is it damaged, but her program is missing large sections of code. She will now respond to any commands I give her main drive. She is called Priscilla."

"Priscilla?" I'd never heard that name before, but it sounded appropriate for a robot that sold luxury items. "What about the other one?"

"Accessing his program now," she responded. After a good few minutes, Maisie's lights blinked around. "The firewall here is resistant and not as badly damaged. I will continue my efforts."

"I know you can do this," I coaxed. With two LiveBots under our control, our chances of success ticked upward. We were going to get Case out of there. I grinned. "Do this for Case. I know you have a soft spot for the outskirt. Admit it."

"I regard all humans equally," she replied. "Save for the one who set me free."

My eyebrows rose. "Are you talking about Daze?"

She didn't reply for a while, then said, "Yes, Daze. He is my primary."

Daze was going to love that.

I'd been gone a short time, but I missed the kid. It was kind of nice having him around—and not at all as annoying as I'd thought it would be.

Maisie continued, "Although I recognize all voice commands, Daze is the only one who has the ability to change and adapt my internal data."

"So, Daze is your owner?"

After a lengthy silence, she replied, "I have successfully infiltrated this LiveBot's program. His name is Julian. The upgrades on his system are more extensive than Priscilla's, and his firewall wasn't as badly damaged." Her lights began to flicker and dance a little faster. "In response to your question, I do not have an owner. I am independent and adaptable, equipped with the highest-grade AI-compatible system, constructed to function intelligently on my own. But since it was Daze who activated my firewall, it is only he who can refine my program. His voice will be forever linked to my system."

I wasn't sure what *refine my program* meant, but we could get to that later. "I can't wait to tell Daze. Let's get back to the bots. Are they ready to act?"

"They will execute whatever commands I give them."

Outside, around the front of the building, several shouts rent the air. I ducked down, pressing myself against the embankment, thankful it was taller than I was. If a craft flew overhead, it might be an issue. But luckily for us, it seemed everything was happening on the other side of the building. "Ask them what's going on inside, specifically near the entrance."

Quicker than I'd anticipated, Maisie replied, "Julian is making his way there now. He has a built-in amplifier and has activated it."

An amplifier? Was that for spying on customers?

Static ensued, then whatever Julian heard was projected through Maisie. "What the hell are you doing here, bot?" a man shouted. "Get back to your position."

"Make him follow those directives," I instructed Maisie. "He has to seem like he's still under their control. Just make him go slowly, so we can hear more."

As Julian moved away, a few different voices filtered through. "Nobody has entered this area," a voice argued. "We would've seen or heard a craft."

"Albert is insisting on a full sweep," a gruff voice replied, getting fainter as Julian exited the area. Albert had to be *the* Albert from the city. One of the people we assumed was in charge of the Bureau of Truth. The same guy who'd convinced Claire he was a loyalist.

I brought Maisie up to my lips. "Tell Julian to find the first location out of direct eyesight and stay there. I need to hear what's going on. Can you turn the volume up on his amplifier?"

A moment later, voices came through, this time a little louder. "Tillman is sending six crafts north," a new voice said, "each covering a separate span of fifty kilometers. If they're heading this way, we'll detect them."

Too bad, guys. I'm already here.

A voice, this one full of authority, started out soft and got louder as it neared Julian's hiding place. "I don't give a fuck what you think," the guy snarled. "This group we're dealing with is smart. That blip we saw an hour ago could've easily been them."

It was.

"We have protocols in place for this," another voice answered, this one older. "Sending your men away from this area is a mistake."

A super big mistake. But I'll take it.

"Tillman." A man who sounded very distinguished entered the area. It could be Albert. "There you are.

We need to discuss getting the prisoner resecured as soon as possible. I think he should be taken out of this facility. They will seek him out first, and it's best if he's not here."

Yes. I will seek him out first.

"We're not taking him anywhere," the authoritarian voice, the one I now knew was Tillman, growled. "My guys will be back with Babble soon. We interrogate him here, and then we kill him."

Not on my watch, asshole.

"We leave his body in plain sight as a warning," Tillman went on. "The longer they think he's alive, the greater threat he is to us." Movement followed, possibly footsteps walking away.

Out front, props were whirring as Tillman's men began to leave—I assumed to head up north to try to find us.

All you have to do is look behind you, dickweed.

Fewer people equaled a greater chance of success, so I was happy to see them go.

"That's exactly why he shouldn't be in the building. He's a threat," the man I assumed was Albert said. His voice carried the appropriate cadence and authority to argue with Tillman. "I agree he should be interrogated using Babble. But we can't kill him. You know who he is. We can't risk it."

Who is he? Someone other than who *I think he is?*

That was a concerning detail.

"That's exactly why he's dying. No other place is as fortified as this one," Tillman said. "We do it here. If they're coming, or that blip was caused by them, we need to be in the most defensible location. After these guys take off, I'm putting the building on lockdown."

Crap. Lockdown would mean the bots, or I, couldn't get in or out without being detected.

"Okay." I held Maisie near my lips. "This all needs to happen much quicker than anticipated. We have to get Case out before they go on lockdown. I want the bots to walk him out of there, and if we're forced to fight, we do it out here, instead of inside." We'd have a greater chance of escaping out here, although I wasn't sure how I was going to get an injured Case back to Luce. Tugging him through this drainage ditch wasn't an option. "Maisie, scan for Seven." They'd taken Case's craft when they kidnapped him. "See if it's nearby."

Julian's amplifier cut out as Maisie's lights blinked. "I've located Seven. It is within ten meters of our location."

I glanced around. "How can that be? The only thing that close is the building."

"That is correct," she answered. "The craft is located inside. I detect a large doorway on the opposite side. There are several crafts parked in a docking station."

That wasn't excellent news.

Having it on the inside made it harder, but at least it was close. "Calculate the odds of ordering the bots to bring Case outside versus us going inside to get him. You know what supplies I have on me, including bombs and weapons. Do a full scan. We'll go with whatever gives us the greatest chance of success."

"Calculating success rate," she said.

She was quiet for a while. Almost too long. I tried to tamp down my irritation. "What can possibly be taking more time than you penetrating the firewall of two retail bots?" I asked. "I need some good news. Lockdown will be starting soon, if not already." Because of my stationary position in the frigid water, I was beginning to lose feeling in my legs below the knees. I began shifted back and forth, trying to restart my circulation.

"Still calculating," Maisie informed me. "Another message from Darby is coming through." Darby's voice came out of the egg. "Holly, what's going on? Lockland and Bender are threatening to leave. You can't win against LiveBots. I'm doing everything I can to try to keep them here, but they won't listen. They're giving me five minutes for you to respond."

"Darby," I said, "tell Lockland and Bender that no one comes for me. Maisie interfered with the radio signal, and they're on to us. They just sent six surveillance crafts north. Lockland and Bender won't have a chance of sneaking by them. I'm in position to break Case out in the next ten minutes. Stand by and wait for my reply."

Maisie answered, "Darby says, 'Will do. Stay safe.'"

The last thing I needed was for my crew to head into danger. "What's taking so long calculating those odds?" I asked.

"I'm evaluating forty different scenarios," she replied. "There are more algorithms to consider, since those forty have similar results."

"Forty? I was thinking maybe there would be three or four," I muttered.

"With the addition of both LiveBots and the possibility of utilizing two crafts, there are an abundance of calculations to make. Such as, if Julian and Priscilla can effectively contain the other LiveBots, or if they carry a weapon or have access to weapons. There is also proximity to the crafts, who is monitoring Case, and how much damage the bombs you have can do."

"Are the LiveBots armed?" I asked.

"Julian is carrying a weapon, but he can't identify it. He's never used it. Priscilla is unaware if she's carrying a weapon."

"How can she be unaware?" I asked.

"Her software is damaged—" Maisie cut off abruptly.

"What is it?" I asked. When she didn't respond, I felt like shaking her, but refrained. The rational part of my brain knew that wouldn't work. "Maisie? What's going on?"

"Priscilla is a newer model," she said, which wasn't really an answer.

"What does that mean?" I insisted. "How does that help us?"

"She…she…she…"

"Maisie, what's going on?" I asked, starting to panic. "We're running out of time, and you're acting glitchy. I need those odds. We have to decide on a course and move."

"I have the calculation for you," she answered abruptly, sounding normal again, which was a huge relief.

There was wariness in my reply. "What are they?" I hoped like crazy that one of the forty scenarios had a projected success rate above sixty percent.

"The rate of success is ninety-seven-point-six percent."

Chapter 9

"How can the success rate possibly be that high?" I countered. That was almost a perfect guarantee of getting Case out *and* surviving—the kind of odds I hoped for on every mission. Those were the kind of odds that kept me alive.

"That calculation accounts for only one scenario," she replied. "The rest are far below a sixty percent success rate."

Even though she was still using her standard modulated robot voice, the hairs on my arms stood on end. "What scenario?" I wasn't sure I wanted to know. If the rest were below sixty, it was the only option, but I knew I wasn't going to like it.

"Priscilla's software is damaged," she said. "It must be replaced."

"Okay." I hesitated. "Then do it…and we'll get on with saving Case."

"It must be replaced physically," she clarified.

"Maisie, I can tell you're hedging. I'm not sure what this is all about. I'm not used to you playing games."

"Humans are wary of LiveBots. It's been well documented throughout the last century," she said. "My programming is purposeful, meant to reduce stress, not elevate it."

"Um, okay. I believe that." I peered at the egg. This inanimate object had absolutely no authority over me. It could not physically harm me. In fact, it was one of the least-intimidating things I'd ever laid eyes on. I'd held bombs in my hand that were smaller and held a greater threat. "What are you getting at?"

"I must replace Priscilla's software," she said.

"What do you mean?" Then it dawned on me. "You want me to insert you *inside* Priscilla. Then you become Priscilla? As in, you'd have a body?"

"Priscilla will become me."

If the hairs hadn't already been standing at attention, they might've zipped off my arms. Suddenly, the urge to sit pressed on me, but because I couldn't feel my legs, and plunking myself down in ice-cold water wasn't an option, I settled for slumping against the embankment. "You're going to have to give me a minute." I had to think. "What…how? How do we…do such a thing?" Maisie in control of her own body caused my heart to beat wildly. I tried to run some alternative scenarios through my mind, but I couldn't come up with any.

"I am instructing both LiveBots to exit the building," Maisie said. "If you choose, you may connect my lifecable to Priscilla's circuit board." She made turning her into a LiveBot sound so simple. "After the task is completed, I will enter the building without detection. Julian will ready the craft known as Seven, and we will fly the target out."

"It can't possibly be that easy," I said. "They're going to see you with Case and figure it out."

"You have eleven hydro-bombs and six sensor grenades," she replied. "As you cause a distraction outside, I will place the grenades in key locations, with the hydro-bombs nearby. Once I have Case and am exiting the building, I will detonate the grenades behind us."

"*Wait, wait, wait.* What?" I gasped. "The plan was to do this quietly. In and out. Grab Case with the least amount of damage and slip away. What you're talking about is serious aggression that would trigger an immediate war. They'd be after us within moments and wouldn't stop until one of us is defeated. Lockland and Bender won't have any time to prepare. That is not what we signed up for. It's not what we promised our crew."

"It's the only way," Maisie said. "All other calculable scenarios have success rates of less than thirty percent. And if we leave him, Case will die."

"Less than thirty? Are you sure?" With my promise to Lockland, that meant I would have to fly back to the city and try this again with a new plan in place. But there was no chance in hell that was happening, especially since Maisie was right and Case's life would be over within an hour.

Incoming props sounded in the distance. Time to make a decision.

"I detect a craft entering the area," she said.

"I know, I hear it," I said. I made my decision. "Get Julian and Priscilla out here." It was the best choice I could make, given the circumstances. I wasn't going to let Case die. Saving his life was worth starting a war. "Then send a message to Darby telling them to expect immediate retaliation and that we have no choice but to go ahead with your plan. Tell them I'll be in touch as soon as I can."

The fact that Daze had enabled Maisie's freedom option was not lost on me.

Letting her take over the body of a working robot meant that she would be free to make her own choices, like walking away from us. That was, until Daze could hopefully set up some parameters.

My ancestors had reasons to be wary of LiveBots. I wasn't familiar with the entire evolution of robots, but things had gone wrong many times throughout history. Humans and LiveBots had had a turbulent past, according to the documents left behind. There had been numerous court cases, which had led to stringent government regulations. Hackers had been an issue. Multiple human deaths had occurred. It was all there.

My gut was to trust Maisie. It was a calculated risk. Part of me was excited to see her in action—after all, she was a trained military operative—and part of me was scared beyond reason. But Case's life was on the line, and a craft was quickly approaching.

Out of the corner of my eye, I saw a small door on the side of the building open and two figures slip out.

My Gem was out as I ducked down to stay beneath the rim of the embankment. "Is that them?" I asked.

"Yes," Maisie answered.

I lifted my head just enough to peer at them as they ran toward us. Julian held on to Priscilla's arm, aiding her. Her gait was slightly off. They were dressed in what appeared to have been nicely tailored clothing back when they'd been built, but it was old and tattered now. Priscilla's long hair bounced around her shoulders as she jogged. It was a mixture of red and brown, a color I'd never seen on any human before. Julian's hair was light brown and cut short on the sides, longer on top.

They were both young, designed to appear in their early twenties at most. Their skin, certainly meant to radiate youthfulness, especially in their line of work, was dull now, which gave them a particularly human look.

"We should move away from here," I told Maisie. "We're too close to the building. It's going to take me some time to plug you inside Priscilla."

"There is no time," she answered. "The craft will land in less than three minutes. I detect Babble on board. The fear and anxiety of the humans inside are spiking." Beneath my grasp, Maisie's secret compartment slid open. When I glanced up, the LiveBots had come to a stop above me, staring down. "Sit," I ordered. "Try to act normal." They did as I asked. I wasn't sure if they'd actually followed my directive, or if Maisie had ordered them to do it. It didn't matter. I began to claw my way out of the water, my teeth clacking as I went. Once I was almost to the top, Julian reached out to help, and I grabbed his hand.

"I'm happy to help you, ma'am," he addressed me. His voice was pleasant and less modulated than Maisie's. Maybe because it was produced by simulated vocal cords. I'd heard that to achieve sounds that were more lifelike, LiveBots drew in air and pushed it through vocal cords that vibrated in a human way. Technology was certainly amazing.

I turned toward Priscilla, who didn't look inclined to speak. In fact, her gaze was positioned somewhere in the distance, her head tilted at a strange angle. She was definitely broken. "Julian, do you know how to access Priscilla's control panel?"

"Yes, I do," he answered pleasantly. For the first time, I noticed he had a taser strapped to his belt. "Would you like me to open it?"

"That would be great." He reached up under her hair, and almost immediately, Priscilla's head fell forward. He must've flicked a switch. "Now what, Maisie?" I asked the status reader.

Daze was going to lose his mind when he saw a real live walking and talking Maisie.

"You must remove her circuit board," she instructed. "Then secure my lifecable in its place."

Sounded easy enough.

I shuffled closer on my knees, my feet beginning to

get some feeling back, which felt like a trillion tiny darts being inserted into my skin. Julian was busy unbuttoning the top of Priscilla's shirt, which was conveniently open to the back, I was certain for this very reason.

The craft had landed in front of the building, and shouting was ramping up. "Go faster, Julian," I urged.

Julian's head turned as he gave me a bright smile, his teeth perfectly lined up and very white. His eyes were lifelike, but outlandish in color. They were the same deep blue as the sky on my wall screen. They made him look a little unearthly. "I require less than one minute," he answered happily. "It's just taking me some time to get it open. Can I interest you in some refreshments while you wait?"

I snorted. His software was highly programmed in the people-pleasing department. "Here, let me try," I said, edging closer. What Julian had been trying to do was access a seam no thicker than a fingernail. It was barely visible. "Maisie, is there an easier way to do this?" I could use my knife, but that would mar the skin. If there was a simpler way, I wanted to know.

"The panel is heat sensitive," Maisie said. "Place your palm against it, and it should engage."

"If it's heat sensitive, why didn't you to tell me to do that first?" I grumbled, complying with her instructions after using my teeth to peel off a glove. Julian had to be as cold as any other robot. The manufacturers had probably made the panel heat sensitive on purpose. Before Maisie could answer, the panel on Priscilla's upper back popped open. I harnessed my Gem and grabbed her by the shoulders, shifting her toward me so I could get a better look. "Julian, stand in front of us and take out your taser. If anybody comes near us, shoot them."

"Certainly," he answered graciously as he stood, brushing off his pants and trying to reorder his hair, smoothing it down on the sides. He'd probably performed that reflex action every single day of his activation. It made me feel kind of sorry for him.

Priscilla's circuit board was the size of two of my fingers.

It contained a bunch of wires and nodes. The board had been constructed by automated machines, and the resistors, memory chips, and power modules were microscopically tiny, and there were millions of them. I gave the circuit board a tentative tug and was met with resistance. "So, do I just rip it out?" I asked. "I can't see inside to undo everything. There are too many wires."

"Yes. Use force to free it," Maisie instructed. "My lifecable needs only one insertion point. Her circuit board is not connected on all sides. It is one of her flaws."

I gave it another quick twist of my wrist, and a few of the wires snapped free. I did it again, and more popped. The thing came out in my hand with a final pull. I tossed it aside. "So, I just plug you in anywhere?" I angled the status reader toward the opening of the panel. Maisie already had her lifecable out. I needed only a few more centimeters.

Inserting my gloveless fingers, I felt around inside. Then, miraculously, I found what I was looking for. A snapping sound followed, and I shut the panel door, scooting back, resting on my knees.

The LiveBot shuddered a few times.

Then, very slowly, Priscilla—now Maisie—raised her head.

I held my breath.

This was, by far, one of the craziest things I'd ever done. I regularly cavorted on cable swings, unsupported, usually fifty stories up. I ventured into precarious buildings that could crash down around my head at any moment. I lived in a world in which one false move could get me killed.

But nothing I'd ever done seemed as outlandish as providing a super-intelligent status reader with a body. It had no precedent. I had no familiarity with LiveBots, which meant I had no idea what to expect. I could be making a huge mistake.

Maisie's gaze pierced mine.

We both stared at each other for a few heartbeats—one beating, one not.

I squinted, leaning forward. Her irises were light green, another otherworldly color. Distinct light flickered behind them, illuminated from the inside. "Maisie, are you in there?" I whispered. "Is that your lidar I see flashing behind your eyes?"

She blinked a few times, her chin awkwardly jutting from side to side, like she was trying to work out the kinks. "It's me." The voice was definitely hers, but it sounded smoother now, more human. "I am utilizing my lidar."

"Can you see? Is it different than before?" Maisie's technology detected things, but I wasn't sure how she formulated a graphic in her mind.

"My software is adapting to the new hardware," she replied as she rose in a single fluid motion. "I see exactly as you see."

Before I could get up and join her, the door the LiveBots had exited banged open and a shout sounded. "Hey, what are you two doing out here? Tillman just initiated a lockdown. Get back inside where you belong!"

I was about to draw my Gem when Maisie's leg shot out, sending me tumbling down the embankment. Her body had been blocking mine, Julian in front of her. As I slid back into the water, my hands scrabbling at the side of the ditch to slow myself down, I heard Julian say, "Why, hello there, sir! We were sent out here on an errand. We will accompany you back inside immediately."

"Yeah, is that so?" the man retorted. "What were you sent out here to get?"

Maisie's voice answered, smooth and unaffected, "We were gathering rocks for Albert."

"Rocks?" The man sounded confused. That made two of us.

"For the cannon," Maisie answered casually. Footsteps came closer. "Allow me to get my pack, and we will accompany you inside."

The guy sputtered, "I don't know anything about a cannon—"

I slipped off my backpack as quickly as I could, pushing it up the small hill as Maisie bent down to grab it.

Julian answered the guy. "They are fine-tuning all the weapons for the upcoming skirmish." Julian sounded cheery even while talking about fighting.

"Go back to your craft," Maisie instructed me in a quiet voice, her lips barely moving. "I will need a diversion in twelve minutes." She turned to go, picking up the pack and flinging it casually over her shoulder.

How did she master acting human so quickly?

"Wait." My voice was strained as I whispered, "We don't know if this is going to work. I should stay. What if you need help?"

She peered over her shoulder. A kaleidoscope of lights shot like pinpricks from both irises. Her face took on a curious expression. One of confidence coupled with something else—something I knew well.

Cockiness.

Had I just unleashed myself in robot form?

I shouldn't have been that surprised. Maisie, by her own admission, had been adapting and learning from us since Daze set her free. Her exhibiting traits like mine should have been expected.

But it was still extremely discombobulating.

My mouth opened and closed on its own.

Maisie turned back to the man dealing with Julian, but not before winking at me. "I will succeed." Her mouth went up on one side, forming a half grin. "See you soon."

Chapter 10

"I can't believe this is the plan we settled on," I muttered, sloshing through the drainage ditch toward Luce, moving as quickly as I could, water spraying everywhere. My entire body was wet. The back of the maintenance structure was coming into sight. I couldn't see the front from here, but I knew the men were likely still inside. "I just followed orders from a robot that used to be made of polymer. One that fit inside my vest pocket and is now a full-grown woman with red-streaked hair and light green eyes."

Unsure if I should continue to follow the ditch—not knowing if it would take me nearer the tunnels—or get out of here, I stopped. Maisie was about to wreak havoc on the building, setting off grenades and bombs. If I could quietly take out the guys here, that would mean fewer people to fight later.

Plus, it would probably be a good way to thaw out.

I pawed my way up the incline, my glove back on,

grabbing at clumps of dirty earth to aid me. Maisie had given me a twelve-minute window. It was going to be a miracle if I made it in time. Rushing through the ditch had taken seven or eight minutes at least. I had four or five remaining. I struggled with my footing, not able to feel my legs.

Once I was at the top, I bent over, water sluicing off my body, pooling at my feet, before cascading back down the embankment. I tried my best to shake the water off as I began to jog across the short expanse toward the back of the maintenance structure.

I heard voices, but they were fading quickly.

"We're officially on lockdown," a guy said. "Maybe I can get my breakfast now."

"Those guys are fools. Nobody's getting in here. If they try, they're dead." Another guy chuckled.

Not dead yet, fellas.

It wasn't a smart idea to engage these guys while they were retreating. That would be a waste of my time and not the distraction I needed. Instead, I took off in the opposite direction, heading toward the mag-lev tunnel where Luce was parked. I wasn't sure I could make it in four minutes, but I'd try.

Running on feet I couldn't really feel was a new experience entirely, but as my body temperature increased from the exercise, sensation came rushing back. "*Ow, ow, ow, ow, ow.*" I forced myself to focus on Case as I increased my pace. He was alive and about to be rescued. That was something. Maisie had said his injuries weren't too extreme.

He was going to survive.

I raced down a short incline, and the tunnels came into view. I pushed myself the last few meters, sliding the rest of the way down on my backside. Luce was right where I'd left her. I hopped inside and had the props powered up within ten seconds.

As soon as I was in the air, I headed straight toward the headquarters building at full speed.

Maisie wanted a distraction? She was going to get one.

I came in clocking two hundred kilometers per hour and, at the last minute, arced Luce in a tight ninety-degree turn, flashing her underside to the upper-story windows. If that didn't get their attention, nothing would.

Chuckling, I immediately raced to a higher, safer altitude. Imagining the chaos happening inside the building gave me great pleasure. It'd been a risky move, exposing myself like that, but because Luce had popped on their radar only a few seconds before I'd made my appearance, I'd reasoned that firing on me would take some time.

And it did.

Alarms sounded in the distance.

In a matter of seconds, Luce's red light began to blink like it never had before, which meant more crafts were within range than I'd ever dealt with before. This plan had better work. As I raced toward the cloud cover, suddenly my most favorite place in the world, I had to decide the best time to utilize my hydro-boost.

I had one chance.

But before I boosted the hell out, I wanted to draw all the available crafts away from the building, giving Maisie and Case the best chance of escape. Once she set off the bombs, some of the crafts following me would turn back.

Glancing over my shoulder, I counted eight crafts in total, all closing in quickly. "*Damn*," I whispered under my breath, thanking my ancestors for outlawing integrated weapons on dronecrafts.

Right as that thought left my mind, a laser blast struck Luce on the right back quadrant. She rocked from the impact, but held steady.

"What the hell?" I shouted. It couldn't have come from a craft. I craned my head around, finally spotting a small, sleek UAC gaining on me. It was the same model as the one that had pursued Case and me in the city.

Crafts couldn't be equipped with weapons, but UACs could.

Especially when they were military grade. This one was quick and efficient, shifting side to side as easily as it could maneuver up and down. It was going to be hard to shake.

Right as Luce's nose hit the wispy white, explosions began to detonate below. They were faint, but I knew exactly what they were. Maisie was executing her plan, and I sent a silent thanks into the ether, hoping for the best.

Punching my radar signals off, I wasted no time activating the hydro-boost.

But I wasn't fast enough. The UAC fired another blast right as Luce shot forward, this one exploding the passenger window. My arms went up instinctively, trying to shield myself from the incoming glass. Shards embedded in my arms and legs as the boost engaged and I was violently launched backward in my seat.

Smaller items whipped around the interior, bouncing off the seats and sides of the craft. The noise of rushing air was so loud, I pressed my fingers into my ears to try to protect my eardrums from the roaring wind tunnel.

If the UAC had boosted along with me, there would be huge problems once I slowed, but I wouldn't know for a few more minutes. At this altitude, I would freeze without a window, so staying up here wasn't an option. I'd be forced to dip out of the clouds sooner rather than later.

After no more than two minutes, with my velocity slowing, I descended out of the vapor. I held my breath, glancing over my shoulder. My heart was beating wildly. I didn't see the pesky UAC, but my relief was short-lived as a blast came from my left.

The front prop was hit. Luce began to wobble uncontrollably.

I was going down.

But I wasn't going without taking that little bastard with me. I drew my Gem and twisted the right stick hard, spinning Luce in midair. With my left arm crossing my body, I aimed through the blast hole on the passenger side, weapon steady.

As the opening lined up with the UAC, I pressed the trigger and held.

With satisfaction, I watched it explode into a million pieces.

There was no time to celebrate. Luce continued her free fall, locked in a rotating pattern. I would hit the ground in less than a minute. The only chance I had to save myself was to try to straighten her out.

I flung my Gem to the floor. To make up for the damaged prop, I had to work hard with the remaining three motors. I pulled up with my left hand to give the craft as much power as possible, while I struggled with my right hand to find the balance required to keep her airborne. I cried out in frustration as vibrations rocked my body, making it hard to keep my grip, my voice drowned out by the air blasting through the open window.

Luce began to straighten slowly, and I caught sight of a large hill speeding toward me. If I could make it to the slope, I might survive. I simultaneously jammed the throttle off with my left hand and punched a button on the dash with an open palm—a button I'd never used before.

Behind me, a hatch opened, and a mended parachute exited, billowing open behind Luce and catching the wind with explosive force.

I had no idea if it would be enough. As the parachute extended, Luce was yanked backward, flinging my body forward. My harness kept me from being ejected through the front windshield, which was nice.

I could barely see as the craft bounced around in the turbulence. I braced myself for impact as Luce's belly caught the top of the hill. Once again, I was flung forward, this time hard enough to crack a rib. The craft slid violently, large pieces of metal and dirt exploding around me with horrific speed, the grating noise like a siren in my ears. Luce began to spin, taking out brittle trees in her wake, each one sounding like an explosion.

I screamed, but no sound came out.

This was it.

I'd imagined my death many times before, but crashing in Luce had been low on the list of things that I'd thought would kill me. Images of Lockland, Bender, Darby, Case, and Daze flashed through my mind at warp speed. Sadness engulfed me. The kid would be disappointed. More than anything, I wanted one last goodbye.

In all honesty, though, I'd had a pretty good life.

I regretted nothing.

Chapter 11

"Holly! Holly, answer me!" a frantic voice called from somewhere below me. Maybe it was above? Whatever direction it was coming from, it sounded hollow and distant and, at the same time, immediate. *Strange.*

I registered the sound, even the voice, but wasn't inclined to answer. Everything felt light—my body, my mind, my emotions. Darkness had thoroughly engulfed me, but I felt at peace. I was fine right where I was.

"Holly, dammit, wake up!"

Case needed to stop yelling. Waking wasn't a possibility. He should understand that. It was dark, I was warm, and this was the way it was going to stay.

I began to drift again, welcoming the abyss.

"The craft is too damaged. We can't get her out without breaking it open." Case's insistent voice beckoned, irritating me because I was ready to let go, but he kept pulling me back.

"We must go back to get the pack." Maisie's voice fluttered around, pinging the inside of my mind. Maisie. She had changed *a lot.* Could a robot have a good life? I hoped she'd have a good life.

The darkness was waiting to shield me from the pain, and I was grateful.

"We don't have time. Give me her vitals again," Case demanded.

"Multiple abrasions. Significant blood loss. Fractured pelvis. Separated ribs. Broken talus. Fractured metatarsals. Fractured—"

"Stop!" Case shouted. The anguish in his voice caused the veil around me to thin, the darkness beginning to retreat. *No, no, please don't go. It will hurt too much.* "We have to get her out and get her to a medi-pod."

"We cannot do so without the pack. We must set off a contained explosion. The position of her craft against this boulder impedes our ability to—"

"Send the guy—the bot. Whoever the hell he is. Send him to get the pack," Case ordered.

The darkness was evaporating at a quick rate—much too quickly. Without it, the coldness would descend. I was scared of the cold. It would expose the agony lurking there.

Case, go away. Please leave me be.

"Holly, stay with us." Case banged a fist against the window. "We're going to get you out of there." To someone else, he said, "We need to shatter the glass. Then we can pull her out."

"As I told you before, it will not be enough to release her." Maisie knew everything. Case should listen to her. "She is pinned from the inside. The front panel and door must be removed."

"Then we'll find a way to pry it off." Case was angry, but I registered the sadness. I felt it, too.

Please, Case. Let me go.

"If you continue to exert yourself," Maisie said, "your injuries will become critical. You are close to harming your—"

"I don't give a—"

My lips moved.

No sound came out. I didn't want Case to hurt himself. After all, we went to all that trouble to free him. He should stay alive. Daze would miss him.

"She's awake," he cried. "I saw her mouth move. She's trying to communicate."

My mind rushed to the surface, and with it the pain came.

The kind I'd never experienced before.

I cried out. I was on fire. Everything throbbed. Fear paralyzed me. My brain couldn't process this. Something would have to give. It was too much.

"Holly." Case's voice was urgent. "Turn your head, away from the glass. I'm busting open the window." He began to argue with Maisie. "I don't care if we can't get her out. I want to…I want to touch her. I need to help her. And in order to do that, the glass has to go."

Pain blinded me. A spray of something hit my body,

tinkling down. Hands were on me. Case eased my helmet off. I cried out.

"*Shhh*," he soothed. "It's going to be okay. We're going to get you out of here."

Using every fiber inside me, I focused on his voice. It was my beacon, my way out of the hurt. I tried to form words, but they weren't ready to come.

Case stroked my hair.

He gently angled my face toward his. So much pain. There was no way to articulate it. My eyes fluttered open, then quickly shut again. It was impossible to function. It was too bright. I needed a tranq dart. Something to stop this. I tried to tell Case I had one in my vest pocket. But the words wouldn't form. All that came out was a groan.

"Holly, I know you can hear me," he murmured. "We're going to get you to a medi-pod. It's going to be okay. I promise it's going to be okay."

"She's experiencing intolerable pain. Her synapses are firing much too rapidly. Her heart rate has increased as her blood pressure has dropped." Maisie's voice was close. "I detect both a pain dart and a tranq stored in her vest. Please use both."

Case complied. Even the lightest touch felt like a sledgehammer. Tears began to roll down my face. "I'm so sorry," Case whispered. "If it's any consolation, if you hadn't sent Maisie, they would've killed me. You saved my life."

It hadn't technically been me. Maisie had physically removed him from the building. She deserved the accolades. I'd only provided the diversion, which had led to this agonizing situation.

"After you give her the darts, we must hurry south," Maisie said.

I couldn't feel Case's hands on me anymore. "We're not going south," he argued. "We need to get her to the city. I'm putting her in that medi-pod, and she's going to be fine."

"She will not survive the journey," Maisie replied.

"She's strong. She'll hang on." Case's voice was feral. "There's no medi-pod down there."

"Her strength will not be enough to aid her. Her body is beyond critical. Her blood loss continues."

"What good will going south do when there is nothing there to fix her?" Case demanded as two needles punctured my skin. The pain was minor, like a bright flash, dissipating just as quickly.

To my incredible relief, darkness began to descend again.

Salvation. No more pain.

With my last bit of my consciousness, I heard Maisie say, "They have one."

~

"Well, then, you don't look too bad by half. This old thing still has some juice in it even after all these years."

I recognized the voice, but couldn't readily place it. A loud grating noise sounded all around me as light filtered down on my eyelids. I wasn't ready to open them.

My head felt like it was caught in a vise. My body throbbed. I felt disoriented. After a moment, my memories came tumbling back. The militia, the LiveBots, Maisie, the UAC, Case, and the crash.

Luce was gone.

I'd fallen out of the sky.

I was alive.

"They got you here in the nick of time, you know," the voice continued. "One more moment, and we would've lost you. I bet you're feeling some pain. This old thing staved off death." A sound like a hand patting metal followed. "But you're going to need something much stronger to make a full recovery."

My eyes fluttered open, blinking rapidly. There was too much light, so I brought my arm up to shield them. Mistake. "*Ow,*" I moaned, easing my limb back down.

"Here, let me fetch you some blockers," the man with the white hair told me. "You're going to need them, and lucky for us, they work like a charm."

"Walt?" My voice cracked, and I took a few breaths. "What am I…*doing here*?" I turned my head a fraction to the side, but all that was in front of me was the interior of a medi-pod. It was rusty. He hadn't been kidding. The thing was ancient. "And where is here, by the way?"

Walt shuffled back into my line of sight, holding a few darts in his grizzled hand, each filled with a different color of fluid. The bright orange one caught my attention.

"You're in my dome," he replied. He looked the same, his tufts of white hair billowing around his face. When he smiled, his eyes crinkled at the corners. It was good to see him. "I didn't expect you back so soon, however. Scared the life out of me when the perimeter bombs went off."

Bombs had gone off? I hadn't registered anything.

I was having trouble piecing everything together. "You have a medi-pod in your dome?" Pain crept in as my brain fully awoke.

"Yes, but it's in a room I decided not to show you, for my own reasons. Here, let me inject you with these. You'll need more at regular intervals, but these will ease the pain a great deal, and one will put you back to sleep." He bent down, brandishing the orange dart first.

"Wait." When he continued, I cried, "Wait!" He stopped, a perplexed look flittering over his features. "Where is everyone? Did they go back to the city? How long have I been in here? I need some answers before you knock me out again."

"You've been in the pod for going on eight hours. Your friends are here," he replied. "Don't you worry one bit. Those LiveBots are something else! Magnificent. Knox is showing them what we've been doing to prepare for the militia and the upcoming war." He'd uttered the word *war* so casually. "They will be back shortly. That man of yours, Case, needs to get himself in here. Thus far, he has refused. I was able to give him something to stabilize his wounds and mask the pain, but it's not nearly enough. According to your super-intelligent LiveBot, the one with the red hair, his injuries could prove fatal if left untreated for too much longer."

Of course Case had refused treatment.

I raised my hand slowly, grimacing, clutching on to Walt's fist, the one that held the orange dart. "I'll let you stick me with those under one condition. You have to get me out of here. I'm not critical any longer. You can put me back in here after Case is done."

Walt's brows creased. After a moment, he nodded. "I'll agree to that," he said. "But I'm not strong enough to lift you out myself. I'm going to give you these and have the others do it once they get back."

I shook my head, gritting my teeth as pain pinged around my consciousness like mini pulses of energy. "That's not going to work. Case has to believe I'm well enough to be out on my own, or he won't go in. Please, Walt. Help me out of here. Then give me the darts." I would welcome oblivion again. As much as I wanted to be in contact with my crew, I knew Maisie could handle it. I was anxious to know what had happened at the militia headquarters, but that was all going to have to wait. The pain ranged in intensity levels now that I was conscious, but every time I moved, it was an explosion. Getting out of the pod was going to take everything I had.

"I don't know about that—"

"Walt, I'm not giving you a choice. Let's do this." I let go of his wrist, bracing both my hands as I struggled to sit up on my own. A guttural roar came tumbling out of my chest.

A flustered Walt dropped the darts beside me as his hands clutched my shoulders, easing me up the rest of the way, making disapproving clicking noises in the back of his throat.

"How many bones…did I break?" I managed between quick breaths, verging on hyperventilation.

"Too many to count, my dear," he replied next to my ear, readjusting me as gently as he could. "It's a miracle you survived at all. The craft was in pieces."

Poor Luce. I was going to miss her. She'd been a steady rock in my life since birth.

"The hill saved me." I sighed, biting my lip to keep from calling out in pain. "Along with the parachute. I can't believe that thing was still operational. It slowed me down enough." Sitting almost upright, I clutched the sides of the pod as Walt reached under my legs and raised them only a fraction.

My head bowed back, and a scream of agony followed. Pain enveloped me, and I almost collapsed backward, my hands squeezing the sides of the pod like it was my last and only lifeline.

The door to the dome banged open above us, and there was a shout. "Holly!" Case's cry was infused with fear. Footsteps plunged down the stairs. Then he was in the room, maneuvering Walt out of the way. One hand stroked my shoulder, another in my hair. His expression was intense as he addressed me. "You're awake. What's wrong? I heard you scream."

I tried to mask my pain. It wasn't working.

Case was a mess. His hair was matted with blood, which was dripping down his neck in fresh red tendrils because of the rain. It must've been too painful for him to wear a helmet. One side of his face was black and blue, his left eye puffed almost shut. His shirt was ripped. I could see an angry wound just inside on his chest, and he'd entered the room with a limp. I couldn't see anything lower, but what I'd seen was more than enough.

Instead of answering, I lifted my hand to the side of his face, realizing for the first time that I wasn't in my own clothes. A large shirtsleeve tumbled down my arm, bunching at the elbow as I gritted my teeth from the movement.

As my palm touched the side of his face, the side that wasn't damaged, Case's eyes slid shut. He leaned into my touch, his breath slowing.

This man. This mystery of a human being. He'd sacrificed himself for me too many times already. "Case," I whispered. "I need you to listen closely. I regret nothing. We took the only option we had to get you out safely. My craft crashing had nothing to do with that. I was pursued by a UAC through a boost. Now I need for you to lift me out of this pod so you can take a turn inside." His eyes flew open as he began to sputter his many objections. I slid my hand from his cheek to his lips, my voice dropping below a whisper.

"If I lose you now, I'll regret it forever."

He pierced me with his gaze. It was full of emotion. My flesh erupted, shivers radiating down my spine. I lowered my hand as his head eased forward.

Achingly slowly, his lips pressed against mine.

Chapter 12

When the medi-pod stopped this time, I was fully awake. I'd lost count of the hours I'd been inside, but I knew this round had lasted at least four. Case had gone in twice, insisting that we take turns. This was my final round. I wouldn't be fully healed because, according to Walt, "This old thing hasn't got the juice no matter how many times you take a spin. Full mending will come later."

The lid opened, and Bender's face peered down on me. "It's about time. We have work to do. The militia's pissed, and they're due to arrive soon. Get out."

I grinned, easing myself up slowly. "Bender, you never disappoint." Various dull aches pulsed from my back and legs, but otherwise, I felt pretty good. Walt's pain blockers were contributing to my overall sense of well-being, but I wasn't complaining. I'd learned in the short time I'd been here that those drugs were powerful and necessary, with the added bonus of making you feel invincible. I pulled myself up and out of the pod. "When did you arrive?"

"About an hour ago." Bender stood with his back against the wall, arms crossed. The secret room where this medi-pod was stashed was fairly small, and no one else had come in. "Maisie and Case flew north until they were within communication range. Darby got the message seven hours ago, and we left immediately."

"How's Mary?" I asked as I took a tentative step forward, testing my legs, distracted by my clothing, which had to be Walt's. The shirt pooled around my shoulders like I'd lost a few kilos overnight. I managed to grab the waistband on the pants before they dropped to the floor. It wouldn't really matter if I lost them, since the top was so long it would've covered me. I'm certain Walt had felt that both pieces of clothing were proper and necessary.

"Mary's fine. Up and around. Seems like she's healed," Bender answered, his voice sharp, which caused me to glance up. His expression was clouded.

"What?"

"We need to talk about the LiveBots." He directed a thumb over his shoulder, indicating that Maisie and Julian were in the next room.

Before I could form a reply, Lockland entered, shutting the door behind him. I leaned back against the medi-pod, bracing my hips and palms against it for support. Lockland nodded once, giving me a head-to-toe once-over. "You look good."

"Thanks," I said, running a hand through my hair.

"I could use some time in the cleaning stall, but overall, I'm happy to be alive."

"Do you trust her?" Lockland asked, picking up Bender's thread.

There was no question that he was referring to Maisie. "Yes." My tone was absolute. "Before we get into this, I want to explain what happened."

"No need," Bender replied, waving off my attempt. "Maisie played us a recording of the entire thing. We get it. That's not the issue. The problem is, how do we trust that she won't go rogue now that she has arms and legs? Human annihilation by robot is a fucking hazard to our health."

None of us had ever seen a working LiveBot before, much less interacted with one. Trina had been my first glimpse into that world, and she was so destroyed, missing skin and parts, that she would never work again, even if she had Maisie to replace her circuit board.

The city before the dark days had been full of LiveBots, but there was no record of what happened to them after the meteor struck. It was clear the government had rounded them up and disposed of them somehow, because there hadn't been any to be found. Rumors were that the survivors feared the robots would rise up and take over, as they outnumbered the remaining humans. So, I understood Bender's and Lockland's trepidation. I felt it, too. "We have a fail-safe."

"What fail-safe?" Bender asked, dropping his arms.

"Maisie has an owner," I said. "Well, not exactly an *owner*. But the person who set her free has the ability to 'refine' her programs. She didn't specify what that means, but I'm fairly certain she's designed to ensure she doesn't go rogue. She is military, after all. They would've been extremely careful with something like that."

"Are you talking about the kid?" Bender asked, his brows rising. "He owns her?"

"Like I said, 'own' isn't the right word," I replied. "But yes, he alone can manipulate her programming. When we get back, we can have Darby write a program that ensures she will never harm us, and Daze can implement it."

"What about the other one?" Lockland asked.

"Julian is a retail bot." I shrugged. "His programming is simple. Maisie breached his firewall, which was damaged somewhere along the line. Right now, she's in control of him."

"She has to release that control to one of us," Lockland said. "Or we dismantle him."

I nodded. "Sounds reasonable to me."

"I don't like it," Bender growled. "How will we know if she's completely out of his system? If anything ever goes wrong, she could summon him to do her bidding. That makes her even stronger, which she knows. The bottom line is that having a robot that thinks for itself is dangerous."

"It is," I agreed. "But she's also an incredible asset. She's so valuable we can't even assign an amount to her. Maisie can access things and enter buildings we can't. She can lead the way into a firefight. She has the ability to locate us and save our lives. The list goes on. So, how about we take this slowly and use our rational brains? If Darby's not confident he can manipulate her programming through Daze, we can reevaluate—"

The door behind Lockland opened a crack, and Darby poked his head through. "Did you call me?"

I smiled. "Listening outside, huh? Come on in. It seems we're having a meeting."

Darby scooted through, heading straight toward me. He gave me a quick hug. "Hol, you scared the crap out of us. When Maisie's messages came through, we weren't sure if you were going to make it. It's been awful worrying about you."

The door burst open, and Daze came streaking in. "Holly! You're out. You're better!" He thumped against my midsection. I'd been able to brace myself for impact as his scrawny arms twined around my waist. "I'm so glad you're alive. They said you crashed." He glanced up at me, his eyes wide. "But I knew you would survive. You're tougher than everybody else."

I chuckled. "I'm not tougher, just luckier. And thankful Maisie was there. She found me and knew there was a medi-pod here."

Daze buried his face against my side, mumbling, "Case was real sad. I was, too."

My eyes tracked upward, landing solidly on the outskirt, who now stood in the open doorway, shoulder braced against the edge. No one else would fit in the room. "I know you were both sad."

Case said nothing, his eyes pinning me where I stood.

"Maisie is so cool." Daze's voice was reverent. "I can't believe she's an actual robot."

"You want to know what else is cool?" I tore my gaze from the man in the doorway, focusing on the kid. "Maisie has someone she's extra close to. Do you want to take a guess at who that is?"

Daze appeared unsure. He bit his lip, glancing around. "Darby?"

"Good guess, but it's you." I couldn't help chuckling at his confused expression. "But with ownership comes huge responsibility. Do you think you can handle it?"

He nodded vigorously. "Yes…yes! I can. I know I can."

Darby looked even more stunned than Daze. "Darb, you're going to have to be heavily involved with this. We need to make sure that Maisie can never turn against us and that she relinquishes control of Julian to someone else. My vote is you." Lockland and Bender nodded. Case remained in the doorway, choosing not to weigh in. Walt shuffled around in the other room. Darby was too overcome to respond. Nonverbal in times of stress was his trademark. We could talk about this later, when he'd finished processing everything. "Okay, now that that's settled, please fill me in on what's happening. How do you know the militia's headed this way? Do they know we're here?"

Lockland answered first. "Knox is in charge of

communication. By all accounts, the militia doesn't know any of us are here. Their intent is to gather as many fighters as they can and then head to the city. They're likely stopping at Case's hometown first, before they arrive here." Lockland tossed a look toward the door, but the outskirt declined to comment once again, his gaze still fastened on me.

I glanced away, flustered, my fingertips lightly brushing my lips as I remembered what had happened between us. The last time I'd been kissed, I'd been a teenager, and it'd never felt like that.

"That gives us enough time to set some traps and get organized," Lockland continued.

"When the militia radioed in a few hours ago, they didn't give this tribe a choice," Bender added. "They said they were coming no matter what, and if the people resisted, they'd attack. No negotiation."

"Do we know the approximate damage Maisie inflicted on their headquarters?" I asked. "She set off multiple bombs. We know it was successful, because Case is here." I inclined my head without actually looking in his direction. "It would be nice to understand what we're dealing with and how many to expect."

"We have no numbers at this point. My guess is they're sending a smaller group here," Lockland said. "If I were Tillman, I'd send a few crafts to get the job done. They won't be expecting much of a fight."

"We can use that to our advantage," I said. "If we take them unaware, before they can get a message back to the militia about possible resistance, it could change things in our favor."

"Knox is pretty confident with the perimeter security," Bender said. "Most of them won't be able to get through."

"That's great," I said. "But if the perimeter security doesn't take everyone out, which it probably won't, those who survive would alert Tillman that the people here are fighting back, and we don't want that. That means he'd either come himself, or dispatch a larger group. We wouldn't have time to reorganize."

Bender crossed his arms. "So, what are you suggesting?"

"That we present an obstacle that forces them to regroup, and while they're trying to figure out what's going on, we eliminate them quietly," I said.

"And what obstacle do you have in mind?" Lockland asked.

Before I could tell them I didn't have all the details figured out, Case suggested, "Holly's crash site would work. It has the perfect topography for a surprise attack. Knox can message them that an unknown crash has been discovered. They'll want Holly and confirmation of her death. They'll want retribution for what just went down at their headquarters, and bringing her body back would be a prize. I was there. Maisie did significant damage to the building. As we flew away, it looked uninhabitable from the air."

Go, Maisie.

"Did I crash nearby?" I asked. I remembered the

satisfaction of blowing up the UAC, then spiraling out of control as I engaged the parachute, the ground coming up exceedingly fast. After that, not so much. "I boosted, and the UAC boosted with me. But I was able to take that son of a bitch out before I crashed."

Case's gaze lingered on me before he said, "You went down about thirty kilometers away. It's within a distance that would be believable that the site was detected by this tribe."

"That plan has merit," Lockland said. "Let's discuss it with Knox and see if he has enough people to place this solidly in our favor."

"The crash site is on the side of a mountain," Case said. Sweat prickled my back as he continued to stare, his gaze hot. "Lots of boulders and dead trees to take cover behind. But in order to investigate, they'd have to park their crafts at the top and climb down. It will leave them vulnerable."

"If we're going with this," Bender said, "we have to make a decision fast. If they're already on their way here to round people up, they have to be diverted before they get too close."

Darby nodded. "Let's keep in mind they know nothing about the scientists, and we have to keep it that way. If they arrive here and find out what they're hiding, it changes everything. If the remaining militia descends, we'll be outnumbered and have no chance of defending this place."

"We might be outnumbered, but we might not," I said as I pushed off the medi-pod, already feeling stronger, taking Daze with me, my hand resting on his shoulder, guiding him toward the door. A solid barrier between me and the outskirt. "Let's go consult with Knox and Maisie. I'm sure we can come up with something. Darby's right. We protect this place, whatever it takes."

Chapter 13

Inside the main dome, I was surprised to see more than just Walt and the LiveBots waiting for us. Knox jumped out of a chair, straightening himself. He looked as if he'd aged a couple of years in the short time we'd been gone. His hair was unkempt, and large shadows darkened his eyes. He'd taken his role of authority seriously, and even though it was taking its toll, I was happy to see it.

Another woman sat at a table nearby. She rose slowly, extending her hand. "I'm Vana. Thank you for freeing us from our oppressors. We will be forever indebted to you." She gestured to a pile of synthetic leather on the table. "I've mended your clothing for you." She wasn't much over twenty, a few years older than Gia had been.

"We were happy to do it. I'm Holly." I shook her outstretched hand. "Thank you for repairing my clothing. I appreciate it." I turned toward Knox. "I'm not sure if you overheard what we were talking about, but we need to get a message to the militia before they enter the area. Is that possible?"

"Yes," he said, nodding quickly. "I can take you to our communications area immediately."

"Who's manning the area?" I asked.

Knox shuffled his feet, blushing a bit. "Curtis."

Curtis was one of the men we'd encountered the first time we arrived. He and another man, Tim, had spotted our craft on the way to look for Knox and Gia, who had purposely gone missing. The introduction hadn't gone well. "What about Tim?"

Knox shook his head. "We had to keep Curtis alive, because he's one of the original communicators with the militia. If everyone disappeared, they would've gotten suspicious. We didn't want to give them any reason to come and investigate."

"How are you keeping him under control?" I doubted Curtis was suddenly on our side. He was a man brimming with anger. Walt had used Quell on him before.

Walt came forward, holding up something in his hand. "With this." The dart held a dark violet serum inside.

"What does that do?" I grinned. "Make him think he's a baby?"

Walt chuckled. "No. It causes all his nerve endings to pulse continuously."

I made a face. "That's got to hurt."

"Indeed," Walt answered. "We've had to use it only once."

"I wouldn't want to get on your bad side, Walt," I muttered. "There would be too much pain involved."

"I wish I could take credit for this, but this one is Nareen's," he said, referring to another scientist who lived nearby. "She's always been a whiz at biologics."

Lockland took the dart from Walt and stuck it in his pocket. "Holly, get dressed quickly," he ordered.

I nodded, scooping up my clothing, eager to get back to normal, happy to see my Gem and HydroSol nestled underneath the pile. I picked up both weapons, directing my gaze at Vana, who smiled. "They're in working order," she said. "Unfortunately, your taser was damaged by water. We have one of our group assessing it now, but I can't give you any promises it can be fixed."

"This is more than enough," I assured her, nodding once, before directing my gaze at Walt. "Where should I change? Down in the cellar?" That was where we'd first secured Gia and Knox.

"That's the best place if you want privacy," Walt answered.

I made my way toward the hatch. Case beat me to it, bending over to haul it open for me. He said nothing as I made my way down. But he hadn't needed to. His gaze had said it all, promising that there would be a reckoning between us at some point. My heart beat faster as I hurried to change, dumping Walt's old clothes on the ground. Vana had done a good job. There had to have been tons of rips, holes, bloodstains, and more, but my outfit looked as good as new, the stitched areas barely noticeable. I attached my weapons at my waist and climbed out through the hatch.

Maisie stood in the middle of the room, Daze next to her.

Light danced behind her irises. It was faint, but it was there. Her lidar gave away that she was scanning for something—she likely never stopped. It struck me suddenly how much better she would be now at protecting the kid. They looked perfectly suited. I walked over. "Thanks for finding me and getting me out," I addressed her. "Without your ability to scan, I'd be dead." I was certain I'd crashed where nobody would've found me.

"Of course. My allegiance is to you," she replied. Her voice sounded the same, but breathy and humanlike. Seeing her in LiveBot form, with her long red hair, was going to take some time to get used to. "I will protect you and follow your commands."

Curiously, I asked, "Do you determine your own allegiances?"

"Yes," she said.

"Can they change?"

"My loyalty is linked to specific experiences and cannot change unless I'm explicitly ordered," she replied.

My gaze landed on Daze. "Ordered by your owner?"

"I have no owner," she replied.

"By the person who freed you?"

"Yes."

I addressed Daze. "I need you to command Maisie

to be loyal to us unless she's told otherwise. Make it sound official."

Daze looked unsure for less than a second, then turned to the LiveBot, his face as serious as I'd ever seen it. "Maisie, swear to protect us, all of us in this room, forever."

I was just about to tell the kid that *forever* wasn't exactly quantifiable and he should pick a more definitive time frame—like, say, a week, until we could get something officially programmed—when Maisie replied, "Affirmative."

Raising a single eyebrow, I nodded, deciding to go with it. We were in a hurry. I told Maisie, "You're coming with us. Once we get to the communications area, I want you to record Curtis' voice. Can you manipulate it and play it back, like you did Darby's?"

"Of course," she replied as Darby made a squeaking sound.

"Good," I said, smiling at Darby. "It was nothing nefarious. She used your voice to read the messages. That's why I knew she could do it." I headed toward the stairway that would lead us out of the dome. "Maisie, order Julian to stay here with Darby, Daze, and Walt and transfer control of Julian to Darby, so he's the one in charge."

This would be her first test, and I wanted to see if she would cooperate without an official order from Daze.

She closed her eyes. A second later, Julian stood, seeming to wake out of a trance. He walked straight to Darby, who stumbled backward.

"Hello, Darby." Julian's jovial voice came out in a rush. "I'd like to introduce myself. My name is Julian." He extended a hand, and Darby cringed back before taking it in a brief clutch. I chuckled. Poor Darby. "I will be serving you from now on. How may I be of help? Would you like me to ready the refreshments for the customers?"

Retail bots were certainly chipper. I wasn't sure that was a good thing quite yet. It had the potential to be incredibly irritating, if not distracting.

Darby stammered before composing himself, smoothing his hands down the front of his shirt. "No refreshments needed. You can…stand guard once they leave."

"I will be happy to do so," Julian responded as he reached inside his shirt, producing a small item and handing it to a reluctant Darby. "This is my communicator. If you press it, I will report to you immediately. If you need something, and I'm not within hearing range, simply talk into it, and I will answer."

I smiled. "Darb, it looks like you just got yourself a robot. Be gentle with him." Knox and Bender were at the top of the stairs, everyone else behind. I made my way up. "Daze, make sure everyone stays alive. If the militia comes, send Julian out and stay put."

"Will do," the kid said.

He was handling my leaving well. I'd purposely left without giving him a personal goodbye.

Walt lifted his hand and gave a short salute.

"Travel safely. Since you've been gone, I've amplified our radio signal to cover a greater distance. You may use your tech phones to communicate."

"Good to know," I said from the doorway. "While we're gone, it might be a good idea to start packing up your essentials, including your bio-printer." I was looking forward to tasting more of his delicious food. "There's a good chance we will have to leave this area in a hurry." I stepped outside to see a welcome sight. I turned to Lockland. "You brought the mover drone. Nice choice."

He brushed past me, heading to the pilot's side. "Yes. I figured we needed the space." He opened the door and climbed in. Knox was already in the back, as this craft had passenger doors. Bender climbed into the front next to Lockland. That left me, Case, and Maisie to squeeze in next to Knox.

I went first. Case slid next to me, his body solidly up against mine. Maisie entered last. There was barely enough room for all of us. I tried to focus on the various aches and pains that lingered since I'd exited the medi-pod, not the heat of the body next to mine. I refused to look his way. Emotions roiled inside me, none of them ones I wanted to examine. Now was not the time.

Lockland turned to Knox. "Give us the location of the communications area." He started up the craft and took us into the air. The bigger craft gave a smoother ride.

Knox delivered the directions, and we landed in less than three minutes.

The building was small and made of concrete. Leading the way, Knox opened the door. Inside was one large room. Curtis lay on a cot behind a set of solid-looking bars of steel.

He scrambled up when we walked in, his face immediately clouding in anger. "What the fuck are you doing here?"

Once we were all in, I said, "You're not exactly in a position to ask us anything. But since you did, we're here because we have a job for you."

Before he could object, Lockland brought out the dart that he'd received from Walt, striding purposefully up to Curtis with it between his fingers. If Lockland wasn't menacing enough, the dart certainly was. Curtis shuffled backward, falling back onto his cot. "You cooperate," Lockland threatened, "or we give you this and do it ourselves. There is no negotiation. What's your answer?"

"I'll…I'll do it," Curtis stammered. "Anything. Just don't give me that stuff."

Knox unlocked the gate that kept Curtis in, and the man scurried out, making his way to the only chair in the room, which was situated in front of several microphones. Along the wall and threading up through the roof were cables, which in turn led to antennas. It was a crude system, but it obviously worked.

Bender situated himself next to the sitting Curtis, his arms crossed, his expression fierce. He didn't need to utter a single word. Curtis picked up some headphones and pulled them over his ears. "What you want me to say?"

Knox was all business. "Repeat this exactly," he said, "or you won't just get one dose of the nerve stuff, I'll make it hurt all week." Knox had uttered those words with absolute surety. The kid was turning into a great leader. Gia would have been proud. My heart bled for her for a second. A beautiful life, gone far too soon. "We've located a crash forty kilometers northwest. Debris everywhere. Is it one of yours?"

Curtis repeated the missive into a microphone. There was only one channel, and I had no doubt Tillman and his crew were listening in.

Not even a minute later, a voice responded, "What kind of crash?"

"Are they kidding?" I asked. "Someone had to be monitoring the UAC I blew up."

"Maisie may have damaged that particular area of the building," Lockland said. "Curtis, tell them it was a dronecraft. The trajectory marks a direct path from their headquarters to here." We agreed on the way over to give them a location at least ten kilometers in the wrong direction, to give us a chance to get there before they arrived. Then, when they landed and didn't find the crash, they would get in touch with Curtis again, and Knox would relay the right coordinates.

Curtis repeated Lockland's words.

Some buzzing on the line preceded the response. "We'll check it out." A moment later, the voice came back on the line. "You guys better be ready to leave when we get there. If not, there'll be trouble. No more talking. You side with us, or you can kiss your tribe goodbye."

Chapter 14

Seeing Luce in pieces was harder than I'd thought it would be. Maisie had explained that they'd had to blow the back of the craft off to pry me out. There was literally nothing left but the passenger seat and some scraps strewn in between.

Luce was utterly and completely gone.

"We have to take cover," Bender growled as he made his way over to a nearby boulder. "They could arrive any minute."

Knox had locked Curtis back up and dropped us off at the top of the hill. He was probably already back in the communications room, making sure Curtis cooperated when the militia called back. No way could we trust Curtis on his own.

Now that we were here, the five of us should have no trouble taking out the threat, especially if we were concealed.

I glanced around, examining the topography. This really was the perfect place to take someone unaware. Plenty of dense forest surrounded us, and even though the pine trees didn't have any needles, they had enough branches to keep us from being sighted from the air and the ground. Once the militia spotted the crash site, it should garner their complete attention.

A hand landed softly on my shoulder, and I jumped.

Case chuckled. "Just wanted to say I'm sorry about Luce."

"Me, too," I mumbled, embarrassed by my overreaction. "Riding in her was one of my very first memories as a child. I'm going to miss her. To me, she was irreplaceable."

"Once we take these guys out, you'll have your choice of crafts," he said.

He was right, but Luce was a piece of my past, something that connected me not only to my mother, but to the grandfather I'd never met. I'd mourn her like a friend.

"Bender and I will head to this side, closest to the crash," Lockland gestured, passing us. "You, Case, and Maisie spread out on the other side. We wait until they're all gathered here. If some decide to wait at the top, you guys take them. The trees should give you decent cover."

"Sounds good." I tore my gaze from Luce and headed in the opposite direction, following Case. Maisie stood off in the distance. I gestured for her to join us. She did without comment. Once we were in the trees, I inspected the LiveBot. "What kind of weaponry are you carrying?"

Maisie nodded to her waist, lifting up her shirt, which was in rough shape, tattered and stained. We'd have to get her some new clothing soon. Two guns were attached to a belt she must've picked up along the way.

I leaned forward. "Where did you get a Pulse?" The other one looked to be some kind of air gun, a little smaller than my HydroSol. Once a bullet exploded into a person's bloodstream, it created air pockets large enough to blow up a heart. But the Pulse was more concerning. I glanced at her, alarmed. "Do you know how to use these?"

"I am well-versed in handling a weapon," Maisie answered, which was completely strange, since she'd been an inanimate object less than a day ago. "And you are correct, it is a Pulse. I had a variety of weapons to choose from, but this one is the most effective. There is no way to survive once the serum penetrates the system. The body begins to decompose instantly. All bio matter is reduced to a liquid state, causing the organs to—"

I held up a hand. "Yes, yes, we know how it works. And I realize it's effective, and also disgusting." I gestured to Case. "Did you witness Maisie use either of these weapons when she broke you out?"

He shook his head, his mouth upturned in amusement, his eyes doing that crinkle thing at the corners. The opposite of the tightening thing they did when he was angry. "No. I was too busy being carried over the shoulder of the other bot."

"I have no idea why you think this is funny," I said. "We have a LiveBot who used to be a polymer egg a ridiculously short time ago and is now carrying a Pulse that could melt either of us into a pool of our own goo with one stray shot."

"I will not make a mistake," Maisie asserted. "My software and sensing ability enable me to triangulate my target more accurately than any human. I can instantly anticipate movements based on a complex trajectory algorithm, which makes my accuracy rate ninety-nine-point-eight percent, even from a great distance and when the target is moving."

I gave her a once-over, my gaze skeptical. "What if I were to accidentally fall into your line of fire?"

"Then I would not shoot," she replied.

"You can make decisions that quickly?"

"My decisions are not based on human emotion or guesswork," she replied. "They are based on instantaneous calculations, which can be augmented as needed. I am no threat to you."

Props sounded in the distance.

We hurried to take cover. "Maisie, head up the slope five meters," I ordered. "Case, you go down. I'll stay in the middle. Wait for my signal. We might be able to shoot from here without having to expose ourselves." Maisie went immediately, but Case lingered. I arched an eyebrow at him. "What? Go take your position."

He leaned forward abruptly, his head bowing intimately toward mine.

I gasped, backing away.

He chuckled, turning to leave. "Just checking."

"What's that supposed to mean?" I called after him, grumbling about dumb men under my breath.

"You're clearly in no state to discuss this matter," he answered, still chuckling.

"I'll give you something to discuss," I growled as he left hearing range. I positioned myself behind a large tree trunk. "What? You think one kiss and we're together?" I made a face as I continued to mutter to myself. "One kiss and it has to mean something? One kiss and we have to *discuss* our feelings?" I didn't want to admit it to anyone, much less myself, but it *had* meant something. I just wasn't sure what yet. I'd never experienced a kiss like that in my entire life, and just thinking about it made my lips tingle in an alarming way.

In our world, romance wasn't something that happened.

Yes, couples got together. They procreated and helped each other survive. But it was nothing like what I'd read about before the dark days, when our ancestors devoted time to trying to woo a mate by giving gifts and going out for pleasure to entertainment venues. Spending time together that didn't involve basic survival was a mystery to me, and completely out of my realm of comfort.

None of us had intimate partners. Not Bender, not

Lockland—not even Claire. There was simply no time for that. Love was impractical.

Love? *Where the hell did that come from?*

I didn't love Case.

Okay, I might love him like I loved Bender, Lockland, Darby, and the kid. Love meant you'd sacrifice your life for another. I'd already proven I was willing to do that to save Case. But that didn't mean it was *love* love.

Thankfully, the approaching crafts put me out of the misery of examining emotions I wasn't interested in wrestling with. Time to focus on the task.

It hadn't taken long for them to figure out they were in the wrong place and get the correct location from Knox. Within moments, four dronecrafts touched down at the top of the hill.

We had no visuals once they landed, but shouts issued shortly after, alerting us that they were out of their crafts. Four drones meant at least eight militia members. I hoped they'd all come down to investigate the crash site, but it was unrealistic to think they all would.

A few minutes later, three men popped into view as they started down the slope. Only three. That meant five had stayed above. I turned and gestured to Case as I made my way toward Maisie, staying low, ducking behind trees. We had to get into position to shoot at the same time Lockland and Bender opened fire. If we were delayed, it would give the men at the top a chance to aid their friends, call for help, or leave. All unacceptable outcomes.

Lockland would anticipate our need to move and would stall until the last possible moment, allowing us to get in place.

The three of us made our way up quietly, passing the men who were not bothering to take inventory of their surroundings, their attention focused solely on the crash as they shouted their opinions to the guys waiting above about what had happened. That this was an ambush hadn't even entered their minds, as they'd spotted no crafts in the area.

It was a brilliant plan.

Case was good at strategy. I had to give him that.

Lucky for us, there were several large boulders situated after the tree cover ended. We ducked behind them. I ventured a look beyond. The men at the top were spread out between two crafts. Three in front of one, two leaning against another.

Their attention was solidly focused on their friends below. I could just make out what they were saying.

"Nobody survived that shit," one guy said.

"Do you think it was her?" another asked.

"Just because Gordie thought he saw that girl from the city doesn't mean it was her. We have no confirmation," another one answered.

"It wasn't just Gordie. It was Newt and Bailey, too," a heavyset man said, walking over from the other craft. "It was her. She's the one who sent the bot in. They launched their best UAC after her, and she blew that fucker up."

"Nobody knows that for sure—"

A shout came from below. "There's no body!"

"That's our cue," I whispered.

Before I could move, Maisie stood, exposing our position. Her Pulse and air gun were out in front of her.

The men took notice all at once, scrambling for their weapons.

I was about to follow Maisie when Case yanked me back, both of his arms pressing me against his chest. "What are you doing?" I hissed. "We have to help her! There are five of them—"

Shots were exchanged.

I elbowed Case in the gut until he let me go, peeking over the boulder in time to see Maisie stride forward like she owned the world. Her back was straight as she fired both guns. Two men were already on the ground, one convulsing, one oozing. As the others returned fire, she dodged each bullet like she knew exactly where they were coming from, which she probably did.

The three remaining men fell in quick succession.

"Oh my..." I trailed off, my gloved hands gripping the side of the wet boulder. She was incredible. I'd never seen anyone move like that.

When it was over, we both stood. "See?" Case murmured. "She doesn't need our help."

"Well, that's abundantly clear *now*," I said. "But, honestly, I don't know whether to be impressed or embarrassed that we human beings are so lacking."

"There's nothing to be embarrassed about," he replied.

"Robots like her are programmed to be superior killing machines."

I turned, making a face. "She was an *egg* a day ago. That doesn't equate in my mind to her becoming"—I gestured toward Maisie, at a loss for words—"that. Plus, she never alluded to the fact that she's a killing machine. She told me she's specialized for combat missions, not a soldier."

From below, Bender's voice bellowed up, "Everyone okay?"

I moved toward the crest and gave him a thumbs-up. "Yep. Um…Maisie took care of it." Bender and Lockland hurried up the hill. Maisie stood unmoving, seeming to stare off into the distance. I approached her. "Are you okay?" I debated putting my hand on her shoulder, but thought better of it.

Her head cocked in my direction. "Of course."

I glanced at the ground around us, my eyes veering away from the three men who had been hit by her Pulse. The other two didn't look nearly as bad. "That was pretty impressive shooting. I've never seen anything like it."

"Thank you," she answered.

"You never even flinched," I said.

"My body does not produce uncontrolled movements. My internal processor can calculate two hundred zettaflops per second. These men did not pose a threat."

"Good to know," I said as Bender and Lockland joined us.

"Did she do all this?" Bender asked.

"Yes, and I'm pretty sure she did it in less than three seconds," I replied. "She walked straight into the fray, spine upright. All her shots hit their targets."

Lockland nodded as he bent over a body. "They've all been shot in the forehead in exactly the same spot."

A beep went off inside one of the men's pockets, followed by a yell coming from a tech phone. "Bombs! They have bombs!"

"*Damn,*" I swore. "The group must've split up." That meant some of Tillman's men had gone directly to the tribe. "We've got to get back there."

"We each take a craft," Lockland shouted as he ran.

I jumped into the nearest craft. "Maisie, get in." She climbed into the passenger seat, and we took off after Bender.

Chapter 15

Knox had given us directions on how to avoid the perimeter protection they had set up. There were only a few places a craft could slip through without activating rocket launchers.

On the way in, I spotted debris from at least two crafts. They clearly hadn't known the path.

"Maisie, do you detect any crafts, other than the ones we are operating, in the vicinity?" I asked.

"Yes," she said. "There is a single craft heading north."

"Crap," I muttered. "That means Tillman's about to know this tribe is retaliating. He'll be back with reinforcements sooner than later, and we're not prepared to fight a large group here." We would have to be ready shortly. We had no choice.

"I detect enough artillery and weapons in the area to provide adequate resistance," Maisie said. That was a relief.

I brought the craft down by the others. Lockland was already out, heading into the communications area. Maisie and I entered the building, followed by Bender and Case.

"Three crafts approached the area," Knox announced as we gathered inside. "Unfortunately, one was at least a kilometer behind the other two. When its passengers spotted the explosions, they retreated. I didn't have a chance to shoot them down."

"Has there been any further communication?" Lockland asked.

Knox shook his head. "They haven't reached out yet. But I'm expecting they will soon."

Curtis sat in the chair, looking glum. "You've rained fiery hell down around us. I hope you're happy," he sneered. "When Tillman arrives, he'll kill everyone."

"Their numbers have been greatly reduced," I retorted. "We just have to make sure we're ready."

Case said, "When they call, we tell them it was a mistake and that we're going to surrender. Give them the coordinates to get inside cleanly."

I nodded. "Knox gives them the correct route—the most advantageous entry point we have—and explains that when the first crafts came through, the perimeter couldn't be disarmed quickly enough, because they hadn't given the tribe adequate warning. Tillman doesn't know about the scientists and doesn't know we're here. With those two things working in our favor, there's a possibility we can take them unaware and finish this once and for all."

Curtis sputtered, "Tillman's not stupid. He's a mastermind. He'll come in here armed to the hilt."

"That's a risk we're going to have to take," Lockland said. "Holly's right. The best we can hope for is to have them enter exactly where we want them, and we'll be waiting."

Bender turned to Knox. "What's the most defensible location you have?"

"Probably Jorgen's residence," he answered. "He was paranoid somebody was going to take him down, so he had areas around his residence equipped with micro-bombs. We've dismantled them since he's been gone, but they can be reinstalled. We can also disarm the launchers along the border in that vicinity, so nothing will blow upon entry. Tillman will have a clear place to land."

"Jorgen sounded like he was an excellent leader." My tone was heavy on the sarcasm. "This is going to work." I glanced around the group. "It won't take Tillman long to arrive once they call. I can't imagine they have many people left. If Knox rearms the bombs by the residence, and we stay hidden until the opportune time, we can do this. You guys saw what Maisie just did."

Lockland addressed Knox. "There are three crafts available for you to use. Round up the tribe members who can't fight and take them somewhere safe until this is over. You have a lot of children here, correct?"

"Yes," he said. "We have quite a few."

"Get them outside of the zone around Jorgen's

residence, then rearm those bombs and meet us at Walt's dome."

"Will do. What about him?" Knox glanced at Curtis. "We can't leave him here alone. Tillman is likely going to contact us while I'm gone. He could give us away."

"He won't be alone." Lockland gestured to Maisie. "Meet our LiveBot, Curtis. She just killed five armed men in less than a minute and won't hesitate to tear your head from your body." He peered down at the man quaking in his chair. "You give Tillman and his men the coordinates to come in by Jorgen's residence. If you don't, you die. Do you understand?"

Curtis nodded so frantically, his jaw clattered. "I understand."

To Maisie, Lockland said, "Don't let him move from this seat. Record everything he says. If Tillman calls, Curtis is to direct him in. If he doesn't, kill him and use his voice to complete our directives. Are we clear?"

"Your orders are clear," Maisie replied.

Bender headed for the door. "Let's go."

Once outside, Knox moved toward a craft. "I'll send people to grab the two other crafts shortly."

Bender and Lockland got into the mover drone. Lockland said, "We're going to go inspect the area around Jorgen's residence." He looked between Case and me. "You two head back to the dome with Walt. We'll meet up there."

Both crafts took off, leaving Case and me standing together.

Awkwardly, I gestured to the better-looking of the three remaining crafts. All of them were pretty banged up, but this was an M class, while the others were Cs. "Let's take this one. I'm flying."

Case said nothing until we were both buckled in and the props were spinning. "Let's head out toward the sea and make our way to Walt's that way," he suggested. "It's the safest route to avoid any issues."

I nodded, angling the craft toward the crashing ocean in the distance. Case cleared his throat to speak again, and I cringed. Before he could say anything, I blurted, "Listen, Case. I know we shared a moment." A searing kiss that might or might not have branded me. "I don't regret it. But that doesn't mean I want to talk about it. Or that I'm ready to do anything about it. I'm just…not."

He was quiet for two seconds. "I wasn't going to bring that up, but since you have, I think we should discuss it."

"No fair," I complained. The ocean filled the windshield, the waves crashing with explosive force, the sounds vibrating like drumbeats through my chest. "I just said I *don't* want to talk about it."

"You don't regret it." It was a statement, not a question.

"No."

"I don't either."

"I didn't think you did," I said. "You were the one who initiated it."

"No, I didn't," he said. "You did."

My gaze shot to his. I was ready to argue until I saw the crinkling at the corners of his eyes. "That's really funny. I'm glad you're so relaxed that you can repeatedly crack jokes at my expense."

"It wasn't a joke. You did start it. Your hands were all over me."

"No, they weren't." Were they? I didn't remember.

"You were beckoning me."

I snorted. "I've never beckoned anyone in my entire life."

"Your voice was soft and hushed."

"Of course it was!" I exclaimed. "I was delirious from the pain."

The top of Walt's dome came into view, and I decelerated. The craft handled fairly well, but wasn't nearly as smooth as Luce, and the interior was beat-up. Whoever had flown it hadn't taken care of it.

Seven, which Maisie had used to shuttle Case and Julian out of the militia headquarters, was parked outside the dome. At least it hadn't been destroyed. I had a fondness for Seven.

Julian stood outside, a large weapon in hand.

"He'd better remember us," I muttered, filling the void since Case hadn't decided to come back with a witty retort. "I don't feel like getting shot at." I set the craft down and turned off the motors. Julian waved enthusiastically. I waved back, feeling silly. "He seems to recognize us." I opened the door. When Case didn't make a move to join me, I turned. "Are you coming?"

Case was positioned casually, his back resting against the door, his right arm braced along the frame. He looked at ease and mildly happy. I wasn't used to seeing the outskirt like this. It was a brand-new Case. "I'm willing to wait."

"Wait for what?" I asked as I got out of the craft. When my foot hit the ground, my left leg buckled and I winced, catching myself before I could fall. Too much action. That, and Walt's blockers were wearing off. Aches began to throb in my shoulder and hip.

Case scrambled out of the craft, hustling around the front. "Are you in pain?" Before I could object, he slid an arm around my waist, taking on my weight.

"I don't need your help, I'm fine," I said as I tried to pull away. The outskirt being this close was making me sweat.

He held on. "The hell you are. Once we get inside, Walt can give you some more pain medicine and something to eat."

I allowed him to lead me toward the dome, my mouth salivating at his mention of real food. A chocolate cupcake would make everything right again. "You're acting like my mother when I was five."

Case snorted as we passed Julian, who stepped aside, booming, "Welcome back! Is there anything I can do for you?"

I gritted my teeth. "No, we're good. Thanks."

"Hopefully, Darby can program some nasty words into his database," Case said.

"I'm fairly certain Julian will find a way to make

nasty words sound nice." I chuckled as we made our way into the dome. I had to admit that this new rapport with Case felt nice. I wasn't sure what he'd meant when he said he'd wait, but I was relieved he'd decided to drop the kiss conversation.

Daze jumped out of his seat as we came down the stairs. "You're back! We heard bombs go off. Why are you limping? Did someone shoot you?"

"No, I didn't get shot. Just pain from the other injuries," I assured him. He refrained from launching himself at me, and I was grateful. I mussed up his hair as I passed, heading toward the seat he'd just vacated. Darby and Walt were standing near the bio-printers. "Walt, when you get a chance," I called, "I need some of those pain blockers."

"Glad to see you're back in one piece," the old man said as he brought some darts over. "Here you go." He handed me all three.

I wasted no time jabbing them into my thigh.

Darby stood next to him, holding a cupcake. "Holly, this place is amazing." His voice came out hushed, with an appropriate amount of reverence. "There's so much technology here. We can do so much to help the city." He handed me the food.

I bit into it, moaning over the soft consistency and sweet flavor as it melted over my tongue. "I knew you'd like it." My mouth was fairly full. "Once the city is safe, we'll transport everything up there. It will take a few trips, but we'll get it done."

Case helped himself to a cupcake and joined us.

Walt picked up more darts from a nearby table and returned with a stern look on his face. "You must administer these once every hour," he instructed me, "or the pain will catch up to you. And you mustn't be too overactive, or you could snap one of your newly mended bones. They're not at full strength yet by any means."

I took the proffered darts, one nuclear orange, one yellow, one blue, and stuck them in my vest pocket. The pain had already receded from my recent injections. "I'll try to take it easy, but no promises."

Walt shook his head. "You are a rare breed, my dear. Afraid of nothing, and pain is your friend."

"I wouldn't go that far," I said, popping the last of the cupcake into my mouth. "I'm not a fan of pain." I swiped at a few crumbs as they tumbled down my shirt. "I've just gotten used to dealing with a certain level my entire life."

Darby pulled up a chair. "Did Tillman's men come looking for the crash?"

"They did," I said. "Four crafts touched down. Bender and Lockland took out three of the men, and Maisie took out the other five. She was insanely good at it. Like, scary good. She's with Curtis right now, making sure he does his job. We're expecting a call from Tillman any minute now. We're going to tell him we surrender and lead him to Jorgen's residence, as a trap. Bender and Lockland are checking it out now." I glanced around the dome and saw that they'd packed up some things. "You might be safe here, but just to be sure, Knox is going to shuttle you guys to a better location until this is all over. Take along anything critical."

"Can I come with you?" Daze asked.

I shook my head. "As much as we could use your help, kid, we've got it covered. We have no idea how many of Tillman's men are left, but we have to be prepared for whatever comes next. Tillman's pretty smart, from what we can gather. We're going to have to try to think like he would."

The kid's head bobbed up and down. "If he's smart, he won't fly in here. He'll wait and see."

"He might do that." I grinned. "Maybe he'll send a few of his guys in first to check the situation out."

"I bet he sends LiveBots," Daze said. "You said he had a bunch of them. He would send them, because they won't lie to him."

"How'd you get so smart?" I asked. "I bet he does send in LiveBots. It's a good thing we have a few on our side, too."

"I wouldn't show him our LiveBots right away," Daze cautioned. "He'll recognize them. Then he'll know you're here and survived the crash. It's better to let him think it's just the tribe."

I found myself nodding along as Darby handed me another cupcake. "All good points, kid. You're turning into an excellent strategist. Must be that big brain of yours. You and Case will make a great team." I directed a quick gaze at Case. "The outskirt's pretty good at strategy, too."

Daze's chest puffed out. "I like trying to think like someone else. It makes life interesting."

"That it does," I agreed.

The door above us banged open. Bender entered the dome, his voice booming. "Tillman's on his way."

Chapter 16

Tillman's imminent arrival hadn't given us much time. We were positioned around Jorgen's residence, a tired-looking structure composed of steel and several large hunks of concrete. We'd taken Daze's advice, and the LiveBots were out of sight, but armed and on the lookout. Curtis had been locked back in his cell, and Knox and two other men from the tribe were waiting out in the open for the crafts to land.

I could tell Knox was nervous, but he was doing a good job of masking it.

Heading into battle when you'd never really fought before was intimidating. This tribe was remote, rumored to be the last outpost before seawater swallowed the land farther south. The tribe had been taken over by a smaller militia several years ago and had no reason to fight. That, and the scientists had made sure they had excellent perimeter protection. For his entire life, Knox had been insulated and safe here.

Thinking about how far Knox had come made me think of Gia.

She would've enjoyed this showdown immensely. Walt thought I was fearless, but Gia was born that way.

Props sounded in the distance.

Case, Bender, Lockland, and I were situated out of sight. Several bombs could be set off by a remote that Knox carried in his pocket. It was too much to hope that Tillman and all his men would converge at once, even though Curtis had told them that the first two crafts blowing up had been a mistake and that the tribe wouldn't resist joining forces with his group.

Tillman hadn't said anything one way or another, other than he was sending a few crafts in. He was taking it slow, which wasn't surprising. By this time, he should be suspicious that the men who died on the hill hadn't been in contact. If he was a good leader, he'd be extra cautious, just as Daze predicted he would be.

A few minutes later, the props were barely louder. "Those have to be the slowest crafts in humanity," I complained.

"Two crafts are approaching at sixty kilometers per hour," Maisie stated from her position a few meters away. She was crouched behind a small structure used for storage. I could see her clearly from my position behind a large chunk of debris left over from some sort of wall. "They're scanning the area with radar."

"They're not going to find much," I replied. "Remember, you don't come out until you're summoned."

"I have retained that order," Maisie said. I could see the light behind her irises flashing. "I detect two humans and two LiveBots, one of each in each craft."

At least they weren't bringing an army of LiveBots.

Two meant we'd be evenly matched. Well, actually not. The odds were tipped in our favor, since Maisie wasn't a retail bot. She was the equivalent of a military specialist soldier trained for combat.

That probably equaled nine to ten retail bots—if not twenty.

The crafts finally arrived, setting down ten meters south of where Knox and the two men stood.

Four figures exited. I could tell by their movements which two were LiveBots. One of the human pilots was bulky and walked with an unusual limp. Once he was in front of Knox, he ripped off his helmet and tossed it to the ground. It rolled with a clatter, splashing through a few small puddles before it came to a stop.

I gasped so loudly I had to muffle the sound with the inside of my arm. "Freedom?" I hissed. How in the hell had Tillman enlisted Case's sustainee brother so quickly? Or had this been in the works for a while?

This was going to be a problem. Freedom was highly volatile and extremely unpredictable. He also bordered on childlike because of a brain injury caused by falling debris. There would be no redirecting him.

No additional crafts were visible, and I couldn't hear any other props.

Well played, Tillman. Send in people to whom you have no allegiance to do your dirty work.

"You will surrender now," Freedom bellowed, waving a huge Blaster around like he couldn't wait to take somebody out. I'd already confiscated one gun from him that sprayed deadly scrap metal, but it seemed he'd gotten his hands on another.

There was nothing likable about this guy, and he was already making our job much harder than it needed to be.

"We are ready to go with you willingly." Knox started to recite our planned response. "But we have lots of men. You're going to need more than two crafts—"

"Get on your knees." Freedom stomped forward, aiming the Blaster directly at Knox.

"*Dammit,*" I swore. "He's going to kill him just for the fun of it." The only other person who knew Freedom was a threat was Case. I wondered what was going through the outskirt's mind right about now. If we killed Freedom, we would lose our chance to lure Tillman here. It was a delicate balance. We'd have to wait a bit longer to see how this played out, and by doing so, it was a great risk to Knox.

Maisie said, her voice low and modulated, "He is within my sights. I await your command." Her Pulse was out, her gaze intent.

"We can't kill him," I told her. "At least not yet. We need something to stun him, not melt his insides. You don't happen to have a taser on you, do you?"

"No," she said. "But I can easily incapacitate him using my hands."

She almost sounded eager. I couldn't really blame her, since I was equally as anxious to get rid of him.

I watched in disgust as Freedom rambled up to Knox, drew back his Blaster, and smashed it against Knox's temple. The kid crumpled immediately. I was just about to go handle the situation myself, fury bubbling up within me, when Case shouted, "Leave him alone and take a step back!"

Freedom turned on Case like I imagined an animal would, his shoulders bobbing, while his legs alternated aggressively. The depression in his skull from his injury stood out clearly.

I slipped into a better position to back Case up, drawing myself out of my hiding place but keeping low and out of sight, my Gem locked on the madman. I nodded to Maisie. "Get ready. Triangulate his movements, or whatever it is you do to keep him in your sights. If he becomes a threat to Case, take him out."

"What are you doing here?" Freedom snarled, actual spittle, large enough for me to see at this distance, spraying out of his mouth. "Are you with them?" He jerked his shoulder toward Knox, his face in a full-on grimace.

Case lifted both hands in the air. "Freedom, listen to me. This is a bad idea—"

"Where's that bitch you were with last time?" he shouted, glancing around as I flattened myself against the debris shielding me.

The other human with Freedom sensed that this

wasn't going well and began to take a few steps toward his craft. *Shit.* The LiveBots seemed agitated, too.

It seemed clear Freedom was acting on his own.

We had to stop the other guy from leaving. If he got back in his craft, this would be over.

Case noticed what was happening and whistled low, getting the guy's attention. "Hey, Tillman sent you here to pick us up, right?"

It took a second for the guy to realize Case was addressing him. He nodded.

"Then could you get this guy under control?" Case asked, angling his head at Freedom. "We're ready to go with you. We're not here to fight. But we're going to need more than two crafts."

"Bullshit!" Freedom roared. "There's no way my brother's with these guys. He's lying."

Shut up, Freedom. You're ruining everything. Now is not the time to be intuitive.

Knox was still out cold. I hoped Freedom hadn't done too much damage.

"Of course I'm with them. Why else would I be here?" Case answered on a growl.

Freedom appeared confused for a moment, before shaking his head, slowly at first, then rapidly, like he was trying to get rid of an unwanted visitor stuck in his ear. Or, quite possibly, chase the crazy voices that had to be a constant chorus from his mind. "No, no, *no*! You don't *do* this stuff."

Case lowered his hands. "What stuff are you talking about, Freedom? I've got a stake in winning the city.

That's how I'm going to make all my coin. You know I never turn down free coin."

Coin? What was Case talking about?

It didn't matter, Freedom's expression changed immediately. "You've got coin?"

Case's hands were down completely as he took a few steps toward his brother. "Not yet, but I have a way to get it. Do you want in?"

So, Freedom was a fan of coin. Interesting, since he had nowhere to spend it or trade it for anything. His tribe was teeny, with little to no resources.

The other two tribesmen who were with Knox remained quiet during the entire altercation. They were just as scared as Knox had been.

Tillman's other guy, the one who'd been edging toward his craft, now seemed to be contemplating Case's words. He must be intelligent enough to know Freedom couldn't be trusted.

"I don't want in, I want *it*," Freedom demanded. "Give me the coin!"

Case smiled. "Sure thing." He pretended to reach into his pocket, then almost quicker than I could track, his elbow whipped up, striking Freedom cleanly in the face. The sound reverberated through the air as Freedom crumpled like he was made of thin graphene that had suddenly broken in two. The thump when he hit the ground was almost as loud as the strike itself.

Thank goodness he was down. I blew out the breath I'd been holding.

After Case took a step back, the guy who was with

Freedom reached for his weapon and raised it. The LiveBots also drew their weapons, which was alarming. "Stay where you are," the guy commanded Case.

The outskirt raised his hands again, smiling, seemingly unfazed that three weapons were pointed at him. "Like I said before, we pose no threat to you. We're willing to come with you. That guy"—he gestured to Freedom on the ground—"was going to kill someone unnecessarily. He had to be stopped."

Knox began to groan, rolling over as he rubbed his head.

The man with the weapon seemed confused, but the LiveBots weren't. One spoke for the first time. "You will get on your knees, or we will shoot." The gun, which appeared to be a laser and a little smaller than my Gem, was unwavering.

The outskirt tried to reason with him. "I told you. We aren't the enemy—"

"Get on your knees."

Case began to comply, lowering himself to the ground.

This wasn't going at all as planned. Coaxing Tillman to agree to come here after this would be a miracle. I picked up movement out of my peripheral vision. Maisie had emerged from her hiding spot.

I swished my hand, sputtering, "What are you doing? I didn't give you the command to leave your place."

"There is still time to achieve our goals. There's a way in, but I must hurry," she answered as she kept moving.

I had no idea if I should follow or not. Having a LiveBot able to make her own decisions was proving tricky. I had two choices. I could either trust her or stop her. Lockland and Bender would assume I'd given her a command, so they wouldn't interfere.

Staying where I was, I decided to trust her and wait it out. Whatever was going on must be critical. She knew the primary objective was to save Case. I'd given her that clear message a few minutes ago. I didn't trust that those other LiveBots wouldn't kill him, and achieving our goals sounded good to me. Maisie was well aware of the plan and had even given us a percentage rate of success. That rate had been only in the low forties, but we'd decided to go with it anyway. She knew we had to lure the bad guys here to fight where it was most advantageous.

I watched with rapt attention as she approached the two LiveBots. Slowly, almost undetectably, one of the LiveBots swung his weapon toward his pal, the LiveBot who had his gun trained on Case. Then, without warning, the LiveBot shot his laser into the other bot, hitting what I assumed to be his circuit board.

The robot fell to the ground like it had become made of liquid, crumpling utterly and completely, limbs sprawled at awkward angles everywhere.

Maisie had found a way into one of the LiveBots' systems.

The other human, the one who'd accompanied Freedom, visibly shook as he spun his weapon frantically, landing on Knox, appearing like he was going to fire.

Maisie lifted her gun and shot him cleanly in the forehead.

He dropped immediately.

Chapter 17

Case stood over an unmoving Freedom.

Lockland had his hands on his hips, surveying the scene.

Bender paced back and forth. "This is a fucking disaster," he growled. "They were all supposed to come, and we were going to take care of this once."

"It was never going to be that easy," I commented. "That was our dream scenario, and since when do our dreams ever come true?" I glanced at Maisie, who had her eyes closed. It turned out she hadn't fully entered the bot's system. She'd managed to nudge the LiveBot into doing her bidding, but was now trying to access the rest of his data or breach his firewall, or whatever it was she did.

The retail bot began to vibrate uncontrollably.

"What's happening?" Lockland asked.

I shrugged. The LiveBot collapsed to his knees, clutching his head in a very humanlike show of pain.

Maisie's eyes snapped open, and she strode forward.

The bot bent his head as she approached. She reached down and opened the compartment on his back, fiddling with something before shutting him up. Then she took a step back. The robot lifted his head and stood in one motion, with no accompanying shakes.

"My name is Matteo. How can I be of service?" the bot asked as he gave a partial bow.

"Damn," Bender said. "We're racking up numbers with the LiveBots. Is this bot connected directly to Tillman?"

"No," Maisie replied. "These retail bots are not equipped to communicate across bandwidths. But this one does have a tech phone and was instructed to call once all was clear."

"Good," I said. "Maybe we can salvage this plan after all. Let's have him call sooner than later."

Knox leaned against a small tree off to the side, recovering from the blow delivered by Freedom, who was still out cold on the ground. "I agree," Knox called. "All the tribespeople are safe. Tillman is waiting. I think we should go ahead with the plan."

Lockland nodded. He addressed Maisie. "Instruct the bot to reach out to Tillman. Tell him the coast is clear, and they should bring in the other crafts, that the tribespeople are waiting for a pickup. Also, tell him there's news about the woman who broke their prisoner out. That should catch his attention."

In less than ten seconds, the bot withdrew a phone from his pocket. He brought it to his lips. "Clear for entry. Everything is under control. Six men and one woman are awaiting transport."

A male voice came through the phone. "Why are you calling us? Where's the crazy guy? Freedom?"

"Freedom is indisposed at the moment," the bot said. I made a face. That wasn't the right word choice.

I nudged Maisie, leaning over to whisper, "Tell them he's relieving himself. Maybe they'll buy that."

"What the fuck does *indisposed* mean?" the voice on the other end of the conversation growled. "Put him on the line, or we're bombing everything and leaving without you. Tillman says time's up."

Maisie reached out and took the tech phone from Matteo, putting it to her mouth and depressing the button. "I'm here," she said in Freedom's voice. "Like the bot said, it's clear. Send the crafts in."

"You didn't give us the code word," the voice complained, sounding more put out than suspicious. I mean, there was no mistaking that the voice was Freedom's.

Without being told what to say, Maisie said, "I fucking forgot the word. What do you expect? You just gave it to me! How am I supposed to remember?"

Oh, she was good.

There was a long pause before the voice on the other end said, "Okay, fine. We'll be there in ten."

That was our cue to remove the bodies and get organized.

The guys dragged the deactivated LiveBot and the other guy to a craft and placed them inside. Case hoisted Freedom over his shoulder and carried him out of sight.

I walked up to Knox and the other two men. "You three can leave," I said. "Go make sure the rest of the tribe is safe. If this doesn't work out, get everybody up to the city as fast as you can. Darby and Daze will know what to do."

They didn't argue, and I didn't blame them.

Before they left, Knox reached into his pocket, withdrawing the bomb remote and handing it to me. "Here you go," he said. "If I wasn't feeling woozy, I'd stay."

I took the device and settled a hand on his shoulder. "You'll be more help to us by aiding the rest of the tribe. If we manage to take Tillman by surprise, it shouldn't require much firepower. Let's hope the odds are in our favor."

"You don't know how many crafts he's bringing in," Knox countered.

"That's true," I answered. "But with the four of us, along with three LiveBots, one of them being Maisie, I still think it would take a lot for them to beat us."

Knox slowly nodded. "Yeah, Maisie is pretty awesome. I've never seen anything like her. She reminds me of Gia—if Gia had been a robot."

I smiled. "Me, too. Gia would've enjoyed this. Now, go."

"Okay," he said. "But I'll stay close in case you need me. We aren't going to let them take us. One way or another, we will defeat them."

"I know we will," I agreed.

"Let's get into position," Lockland ordered. "Same plan as before."

"Can't be the same plan," I said. "I just sent Knox away."

"Why'd you do that?" Bender asked.

"Because he was knocked silly by Freedom and wasn't thinking straight. I have the remote." I held up the small box. "Tillman's never seen Knox before." I nodded at Bender. "You or Lockland can stand in as Knox."

"Fine," Bender said as I handed him the remote. "I'll do it."

"The important thing is getting them into the right position," Lockland said. "They have to be in this area." He gestured to the expanse in front of us.

"I know what the plan is," Bender grumbled. "I get them where I want them, then we blow them up."

"Don't forget we have Matteo." I indicated the retail bot, who stood nearby. I glanced around. "Where's Julian?"

Julian popped up a few meters away from behind a tree and called, "I'm right here!" Smiling brightly, as usual. That bot didn't know the meaning of the word *unhappy*.

Maisie stood next to me. "He won't move without orders, will he?" I asked her.

"No, he will stay put until he is told," she said.

"Good." I waved at Julian. "Get back behind the tree." He did as I asked. "Position Matteo next to

Bender," I told her. "Follow Bender's prompts. Answer the questions the way they'd think this retail bot would respond to them, quickly and efficiently. Can you do that?"

"Of course."

"Let's go." I made my way toward the place where I'd taken cover before. Maisie went to her spot. They couldn't discover me or Case here, or the two LiveBots, or they'd know something was up. Case was still dealing with Freedom. He'd know enough to stay out of sight.

In the middle of the clearing, Bender paced back and forth agitatedly. Holding his weapon would've made this easier, but if he was armed when they arrived, they'd be suspicious.

Luckily, we didn't have to wait long. Sounds of multiple crafts entering the area came a few minutes later.

This was it. We were about to have a showdown with the people behind the secret government agency that had had plans for years to take over the city and kill its less-desirable—according to them—inhabitants. Better to do it here than up North. We had no idea how many people had survived Maisie's bombing, but the militia's numbers had to be significantly depleted. Tillman had a team of at least thirty, and who knew how many of the hundred and eighty-four at the headquarters survived when Maisie broke Case out?

I peeked over the top of the wall and counted eight crafts.

That was a significant number.

Matteo's tech phone went off. He answered it, but at this distance, I couldn't hear the conversation. My gaze shot to Maisie. I was relieved that she seemed at ease. As Matteo spoke into the phone, Bender didn't seem alarmed, so I forced myself to relax.

A noise sounded next to me, and I turned quickly, bumping my face against Case's shoulder. "*Ow.* What are you doing here?" I rubbed the tip of my nose.

"This location was the closest. I didn't think there would be eight crafts," he said.

"Me neither, but we can handle it. Where did you stash Freedom?"

"Half a kilometer away. I didn't have anything to restrain him. If he wakes soon, which I highly doubt, he probably won't be able to find his way back."

That was debatable. "He's highly unpredictable. Do you think it was safe to keep him alive?" I asked.

Case shrugged. "He's my brother. I couldn't kill him."

"Fair enough," I replied. "But if he gets in our way again, he's not going to survive."

"I accept that."

The crafts began to enter the area, one after another.

They landed far enough away from the first two crafts, which was helpful, since there were bodies inside. These crafts were in much better shape than the four that had arrived at the crash site. There was one in particular that looked especially well cared for. It had to be Tillman's.

The doors on the front two crafts popped open, and

four heavily armed men dressed in all-black synthetic leather, black helmets, and gloves emerged.

These were the real soldiers, not some guys they picked up along the way.

The men didn't look like they were going to be easy to fool, which would not work in our favor.

My stomach clenched. "I think we made a mistake," I whispered urgently. "We left Bender out there exposed. They could blow him up before we have a chance to act."

"He can hold his own," Case murmured back.

"What if someone recognizes him?"

"They don't live in the city."

"Yeah, but they have to visit once in a while to check up on things. Reed told us that people came up once or twice a year. Bender's notorious." A sinking feeling crept in. "We've made a tactical error. I can feel it. It should've been somebody else, not Bender."

The four soldiers marched forward, their weapons raised. If Bender so much as reached for his gun, they would kill him on the spot.

The rest of the crafts stayed shuttered, including the X series that I believed was Tillman's. They were waiting to see what happened. Smart.

One of the soldiers broke away, taking a step forward. "Where are your men?"

"They went to get their things," Bender said easily, crossing his arms, affecting the *I don't give a shit* stance, which he was a master of. "They'll be back momentarily."

"Where are our men?" he asked, glancing around.

"They went with them," Bender answered without hesitation.

The man brought his huge laser gun to rest on Bender's chest. The weapon would split him in half with one blast.

Matteo began to speak. "They informed me that they had valuable artillery to contribute," the retail bot chirped in a tone similar to Julian's. "I gave them the okay to retrieve it. This place is known for its bombs, so I figured that was what Tillman would want."

The man began to lower his weapon, but then seemed to think better of it. "Where's the other bot?" It was clear this man *wanted* to believe what Matteo was telling him, but things weren't adding up. All his men should be here, as well as the tribesmen.

That had been the agreed-upon deal.

"If you call some more of your men out here," Bender suggested, "we can get this done a lot quicker. The weapons are right over that rise." He gestured to the left.

I shook my head, gritting my teeth. "No, Bender. That's not going to work. Nobody else is getting out of their crafts until they see your men. They're used to being cautious. We promised them men, and no one's here."

"We're not going anywhere with you," the man stated, his voice hard. "In fact, you're going to get the fuck over here until they come back."

I began to rise as a reflex, wanting to aid Bender,

but Case grabbed my arm, stopping me. He leaned over, whispering, "You won't help him by exposing yourself."

Maisie glanced at me, and I nodded once, my intent clear: *Do whatever you can to save Bender.*

Matteo raised his hand as Bender stalled. "There's no need to get agitated," Matteo assured everyone. "I've taken care of everything."

"What makes you think we'd trust you, bot?" the man with the huge laser gun snarled.

The LiveBot shrugged in a decidedly humanlike way. "Well, because I'm following direct orders. We're here to pick up the tribesmen, and that's what we're doing. They're gathering valuable weaponry to aid our cause."

"You don't know that," the guy argued. "Six of our guys have gone missing. Where did they go, huh? Something's going on here, and we're going to figure out what it is."

One of the men standing behind the guy with the big gun started to wander toward the other crafts, the ones with the bodies stashed inside.

Shit.

"Case, this is about to go badly," I said. "We're going to lose people." Panic that had started in my stomach fluttered into my chest.

"No, it's not—"

Case was cut off as Maisie strode out from behind her hiding spot, both weapons held high. At the same time, Matteo grabbed Bender's Web out of its holster.

Maisie took down two of the soldiers as Matteo shot the other two. None of the men had time to react. They all fell where they stood.

I gasped. It had all unfolded so quickly.

My instinct was to shout for Bender to get down, but the words stuck in my throat. The rest of the crafts were either going to open fire on us or leave the scene. I had no idea which it was going to be.

Maisie and Matteo both had their guns aimed at the X craft. Maisie seemed to know what was going to happen.

And, sure enough, painfully slowly, the pilot door opened.

I held my breath. A massive thigh emerged, followed by an equally large torso. Both were covered in black synthetic leather. If this was Tillman, he was a huge man. Before he was all the way out, he reached back inside. I heard a scream.

A woman's scream.

Then the passenger door went up, and an older man, with a clipped white beard and dressed in regular clothing, got out. Both men were dragging a body, kicking and screaming, out of the craft.

I recognized the first woman. Helena. Freedom's wife.

The second woman I'd never seen, but beside me, Case made a noise, followed by, "Wendra."

My gaze shot back to what was unfolding in front of us. "Your sustainee sister? They brought hostages?" I was slack-jawed.

"It appears they did," he said.

Chapter 18

The women were frightened and struggling. How had Tillman known to bring them here? And that Case had ties to these women?

There was much more to this story, and we were sadly behind.

Tillman was indeed a massive man. He appeared to be in his late forties, from what I could see of his face, which was partly occluded by a resistant Helena.

The men half dragged, half shoved the women in front of them.

Behind them, all the craft doors opened, and ten soldiers emerged, all holding weapons of various shapes and sizes.

Maisie stood her ground, both guns up. She could calculate a lot, but with that many soldiers, it would be difficult. She wasn't infallible. Based on the fact that these women were obviously hostages, I assumed Maisie would understand not to harm them.

"How did my LiveBots turn against me?" Tillman bellowed.

No one spoke.

He brought out a Pulse and set it against Helena's temple. Of course he had a Pulse. "I know there are more of you here," he said. "If you don't surrender to us immediately, we'll kill these two."

Bender had taken his Web from Matteo. "We don't give a shit if you kill them," Bender retorted. "Why you think we would is a mystery."

Tillman and Bender were fairly evenly matched physically, though Tillman had a slight edge in height and girth. I had no idea if he was bald under the helmet or not, but it didn't matter. "Somebody here cares about them." Tillman snickered. "Isn't that right?"

Tillman had done his research.

But how?

"Nobody cares about them." Bender's voice was razor-sharp. "Do you know who I am?"

Tillman grinned. Everything about the man projected evil. This guy enjoyed pain. "Of course. But you're out of your element here, Bender."

"I have no element," Bender snapped. "But what I do have is a lot of fucking firepower. Just so we're clear, I'm ready to blow this place sky-fucking-high, including myself, before we give in to any of your demands. If you think I'm lying, then you don't know me or my reputation."

Tillman holstered his Pulse and exchanged it for a huge blade with serrations large enough that I could see them from a distance. "Then you won't mind if I carve up this beautiful woman in front of you?"

Bender's plan wasn't going to work.

Tillman knew the rest of us were watching. He knew Bender cared about his family. They'd been monitoring us for years, of course they knew, and by discovering those details, Tillman had figured out the best way to keep us in line. Bringing in Helena and Wendra was a brilliant move, one that proved he'd been on to Case as well.

A solid advantage for us was that he didn't know about Maisie's super-soldier capabilities. Based on his blatant disinterest in her, he viewed her as Priscilla, the broken retail bot. I had no idea if his miscalculation would be enough, however.

As my mind raced, I maneuvered into a better position to spring into action, trying to figure out the best approach. Before I could reason my way to something logical, Wendra began to struggle in her captor's grasp and shouted, "Just kill us! We can take it. Do it already, you bastards!" She fought so hard she almost broke free.

My type of warrior.

"You will contain yourself," the man with the white beard ordered. "I will not abide by this."

Tillman snickered. "You're going to have to control her, Albert. Or I will."

So this was Albert.

The man who had fooled Claire into thinking he was a loyalist. Guessing by his age, he'd been around since the beginning and had played a prominent role all these years. I hoped we could take him alive. Babble would fill in a lot of blanks.

Albert produced a small laser gun and, without preamble, shot Wendra through the shoulder. She fell to the ground, writhing in agony, clutching her gushing wound. Albert appeared satisfied. "How's that for control?" His voice was higher pitched and more precise than Tillman's. By his tone and look of disdain, Albert considered himself above his henchman.

That was likely one of many mistakes.

It was clear there was only one person in charge here. Tillman. He ignored Albert's comment, because it would've been beneath him to respond.

Case had a hold on me, keeping me from jumping up and exposing my position as I watched Wendra roll around on the ground in pain. But I returned the favor in kind. My hold on Case's trench was like iron, rooting him in place. If I wasn't going anywhere, neither was he. Case's face was as intense as I'd ever seen it. Hate radiated outward.

At least Wendra wasn't dead. The crappy medi-pod could help save her, if we could get her there in time.

Bender brandished the remote I'd given him, holding it up in front of him, appearing bored. He hadn't reacted to Wendra's injury. Not even a little bit. "I have a gift for you in the form of a shit-ton of hydrogen." He rocked the small device back and forth. "Why don't we stop this fucking game and you tell me what you came here for?"

Tillman's expression didn't change. He was enjoying himself. He ran the tip of his blade along Helena's neck. The stoic woman kept her screams to herself. "We came here to get rid of you. You're a nuisance."

"And you're just figuring that out now?" Bender snorted. "Why'd it take you so long?"

"We let you live, because in the years leading up to this, you provided us with a valuable service," Tillman answered as a rivulet of blood slowly trailed down Helena's neck.

"And what exactly did we do for you?" Bender asked.

"You took care of any threats, so we didn't have to," Tillman answered.

"Like Tandor?" Bender asked.

"Hardly." His deep baritone projected a threat. "We sent that asshole up to you knowing he would die. If he got lucky, so be it. But it was time for him to go. You helped with other things, like halting minor government takeovers and preventing plots that undermined our authority. We've got plans in place, so your service was helpful."

Realizing that we'd helped these guys set my teeth on edge and made my conscience feel dirty.

"I've heard about these plans," Bender said. "Care to elaborate?"

Albert cleared his throat, seemingly put out by this conversation. After all, he believed he was the one in charge. "We don't have anything to share with you," he snipped. "Call your *family* out from wherever they're lurking, so we can end this."

"Yeah." Bender chuckled. "That's what I'm gonna do."

"You're going to have to cooperate sooner or later," Albert said. "If you call them out now, we may decide to spare a few."

"Not a chance," Bender answered. "Remember, I have this." He waggled the detonator in front of them one more time. "If I press this right here"—his finger lingered over the button—"we all die. And if you're wondering, I have no fear of death. In fact, being blown up is my number-one preferred way to go. I have no complaints." He really didn't. Bender was always ready to go, whenever it was his time. It was an excellent trait to possess in our world.

I shared that same philosophy, but that didn't stop me from worrying about Darby and Daze and everyone else. If some of Tillman's soldiers survived the blast, there would be no doubt they'd hunt down any survivors and kill them.

This would be it for all of us if we lost.

More than anything, I wanted Daze to have a good life—a better one than I'd had.

Albert took a step forward, then thought better of it and shuffled backward. His first sign of uncertainty. "We can shoot you before you can set that off." Irritation infused his tone.

"No, you can't." Bender was unfazed.

Maisie still had her guns up. She would know from their micromovements if one of the soldiers was going to shoot. I took solace in that.

"Waiting this out is going to kill me," I muttered to Case. "It's a standoff no one can win."

"We need a distraction," Case answered.

"We should've positioned people farther apart." But trying to get behind eight crafts without being seen would've been an incredible challenge. We were utilizing all of the cover available in the area.

"No, we're in the right place," he said. "When this goes down, we need to be close and at the ready."

I had my weapons out, but I wasn't confident any of this would be enough.

"He's not bluffing," Tillman told Albert. "I can tell."

The soldiers behind Tillman started to get agitated, shuffling back and forth, not knowing what direction this was going to go.

I spotted movement to my right, my hand sliding down, closing around Case's arm. "Is that Julian?" Julian had vacated his spot behind the tree. I could just make out the top of his head as he crawled, military style, along the ground. I was fairly certain no one else could see him from their vantage point, but I wasn't positive.

We'd find out in a minute or so.

"I believe it is," Case whispered back. "Maisie must have control again."

"Does that mean she lied to us?" I asked. "She gave control over to Darby. We all saw it."

"Well, she's a powerful supercomputer, analyzing the pros and cons all the time. My guess is she allowed for a fail-safe for this very reason. It was smart of her."

"It was, but it won't endear her to the group," I grumbled. "We have to be able to trust her completely."

"This will solidify her place in the group if she manages to save all of our hides."

I pondered that.

Not knowing what the outcome would be, it was hard to decide how to feel. Maisie was clearly positioning Julian. She was controlling Matteo, herself, and Julian at the same time, and it was impressive. That could not be dismissed.

"I guess we're at a standstill," Tillman said, his blade lingering at the soft indent of Helena's neck. "Not cooperating with us now means you'll have to face us in the future. I have more men and more power than you."

"I see no standstill," Bender countered. "You try to leave, I push this button."

"Your bombs won't take all of us out," Tillman threatened. "My men won't abandon their posts. Not only do they follow me, they follow the movement." Albert placed his hands on his hips, his expression a full-on frown. He was tired of the banter.

"Yeah, about that," Bender said. "You seem intelligent enough. How'd you get caught up in all this shit?"

Tillman grunted. "Seriously? You're picking now to get chatty? Bottom line is ultimate salvation is hard to refuse. To finally reap all the rewards in our crap-ass world—who wouldn't jump at that?"

Albert appeared ready to blow. He had worked

himself up so much, he'd begun to turn blotchy. "Our group is *sacred*," he sputtered. "We will rejoice in the new world we will create. With it will come paradise and riches your brain can't comprehend."

"Like the sun shining, birds chirping, and the Flotilla magically bringing back resources they've harvested after all these years." Bender sounded bored. "You really believe that bullshit? You gotta be kidding me. We humans don't have any control over the environment. End of story. We're passive inhabitants in our turbulent world. But even if the sun doesn't shine again in our lifetimes, my family is committed to making where we live a better place, and that includes getting rid of scum." He lifted the remote and made a show of pressing the button.

Albert held up his hands and shouted, "Don't do that!" He was a spineless bastard looking out only for himself.

Bender lowered his hand, chuckling. It'd been incredibly easy to make Albert squirm. "It's going to happen one way or another. Either now or in a few minutes." Bender shrugged. "I can wait."

There was more movement in the distance. I squinted. Darby and Knox were making their way toward the craft at the back, while Julian, who was now out of sight, was presumably heading to the right. I tapped Case and gestured.

"Now we really need that distraction," he whispered. "If we can confuse them for a few seconds, we should be able to take most of them out."

Tillman boomed confidently, "I think you'll change your mind when you see what else I brought with me." His tone rang with creepy certainty.

Hair rose on my arms.

Tillman raised a fist in the air, and one of his soldiers near the back returned to a craft and pulled something out. Something small and crying.

"That's not…that's not a *child*, is it?" I recognized the pleading in my own voice.

Please, don't be a child.

The shape was smaller than Daze. Definitely a little boy. The soldier carried him forward like a loose sack in his arms. Out of the craft, the child quieted, apparently too stunned to cry.

Helena began to weep.

No, no, no. It was Sampson.

The same sweet boy I'd met when we'd gone to interrogate Freedom. He was one of Freedom's many children and no older than four. *Please, please let the other children be alive.*

"There's more where this one came from." Tillman laughed, a deep, throaty sound that marked him pleased with himself. "Some of them little girls are mighty pretty, too. Just ripe for the picking."

The asshole was going to hurt for this. Case's tension equaled mine, both of us ready to explode. Tillman was not going to get away with any of this.

"You expect me to change my mind because you kidnapped a child?" Bender said. "Not a chance."

All of a sudden, angry bellows erupted from the right, several meters away.

Our distraction had finally arrived.

Chapter 19

"What are you doing with my kid?" Freedom roared. Case's sustainee brother stumbled into sight, looking even more crazed, hair sticking straight in the air, sand caking his face.

He was the ultimate distraction.

Bender didn't hesitate, and neither did Maisie.

Shots were fired as Case and I sprang from behind the wall.

As I ran, weapons out, I spotted Knox and Darby as they rushed into the fray from behind and took out some of the soldiers. Albert was down and so was Matteo, but Tillman had positioned Helena so he could use her as a shield as he retreated.

"We're coming for you!" Bender shouted as he stalked forward. "This isn't over."

Tillman smiled, his face barely visible behind Helena's head. "I thought you didn't care about the woman. It seems as if you do after all."

I didn't have a clear shot, and neither did anybody else. Maisie would've taken one if she could've. Then Tillman was inside his craft. He flung Helena to the floor, slammed the door, and started the props.

Maisie fired repeatedly at the windshield, but the glass held.

I brought my Gem up, ready to take a shot, but found myself flat on the ground before I could complete my task. Case had tackled me.

"What are you doing?" I yelled. "Get off. He's getting away!"

Tillman's craft, along with two others from the back, took off into the sky, boosting out of sight.

Case panted, rolling over so that he was outstretched on his back, arms spread. "The surface of that craft was shiny." He took a few short breaths. "I thought the paint looked fresh, but then I realized it was a reflective coating."

If I'd shot my Gem, the bounce back could've killed me and whomever was nearby.

Case had saved my life. *Again.*

We both staggered to our feet. Albert was down, as well as six out of the ten soldiers. Four had retreated with Tillman. Matteo was lying in a heap, arms and legs settled in strange positions. Wendra was conscious, still holding her shoulder. Helena had scooped a tearful Sampson into her arms and was rocking him.

Freedom looked bewildered.

He homed in on Case immediately, his fury radiating outward. "This is all your fault!" He limped forward, his Blaster in hand. He'd managed to find his weapon along the way.

No, no, no.

Case raised his hands. He'd dropped his Pulse when he tackled me and hadn't yet retrieved it.

I trained my Gem on Freedom, my voice calm. "Think before you act, Freedom. Case is not your enemy."

"He is, too," Freedom sneered, eyes wild. "He's always been against me. He's hated me from the beginning!"

Maisie quietly approached from behind him, her Pulse trained on the back of Freedom's head. One wrong move and Freedom was going to experience rapid changes in his elemental state. Darby was helping a likely concussed Knox into the area. Julian entered from the other side, and for the first time, I noticed Lockland, who was farther away than he'd been before, moving toward us. He'd been trying to get to the soldiers at the back, too. His Blaster was up.

We were all accounted for.

"Just kill the bastard and get it over with," Wendra cried. "He went with them willingly! He betrayed us! Kill him, and then somebody help me before I bleed out."

"Do you hear that?" I asked Freedom. "Your sister wants us to kill you. If you stay on your current path, that's exactly what's going to happen."

Freedom didn't stop. He didn't even pretend to stop.

Shit.

He pulled the trigger, and three shots rang out.

"No!" I shouted.

Case and Freedom collapsed at the same time.

My heart stopped. I couldn't move.

Then I flung my Gem down and dropped to my knees. Case was prone. I rolled him over. There was no blood on his face or chest. "Case," I cried. "Wake up." Maisie knelt beside me. "What's wrong with him?" My voice was bordering on frantic. "I don't see any blood."

"He was hit in the abdomen," she said. "Peel his coat back very carefully."

I did, locating a large jagged piece of scrap metal embedded in his stomach. Luckily, Freedom's aim had been off, so only one large piece of metal and a few smaller ones had struck Case.

"Normally, it is not wise to remove a projectile like this until medical attention is imminent, but it's too close to his spleen. The risk of damage while moving him is greater than the risk of removal," Maisie said. "Once it's out, apply pressure to the wound. He must get to the medi-pod as soon as possible."

"You mean, extract it from his body right now?" I gasped, watching the blood ooze out slowly.

"I can do it if you prefer."

I shook my head. "No, I'll do it." Without overthinking it, I grabbed on to the sharp metal shard and pulled. It slid out with an awful squishing sound.

Case yelled, his chest rising as his eyes blinked open. "*Ow.* What the hell?" He glanced down to see the wound, which my hand was now covering, providing ample pressure to stop the blood flow.

"You're going to be okay." I leaned over, my face extremely close to his. "And I swear, if you do this to me again, I'll kill you myself."

Instead of howling in pain, he grinned. Then he slid his hand behind my neck and brought my lips down to meet his.

My eyes slid shut.

After what felt like a lengthy amount of time, I lifted my head, breathless. Case chuckled. "*Hmm*," I murmured. "Not the reaction I was expecting. Care to explain?"

He stopped, his face growing serious, his gaze locking on mine. "When I said I would wait for you, I thought it would take years, not hours. This is a nice surprise."

Before I could complain about his ideas about timing, he kissed me again.

~

"That man took all the children and Lea and Mimi," Helena said. "I don't know where he took them, but they are gone."

"That asshole took them to his harem, that's where," Wendra retorted. She'd just gotten out of the medi-pod and was on a fresh dose of pain blockers, almost as good as new. The mark on her shoulder was still visible, but healed over.

Case had insisted she go first, and now the outskirt was taking his turn.

It took everything I had not to situate myself in the room with him to keep watch. He'd lost a lot of blood and had looked terrible.

Nobody had said anything about our newfound intimacy, but I knew it was coming. Surprisingly, my worry about Case eclipsed my caring about what anyone had to say on the matter. Denying how I felt any longer was pointless. Case and I were a team, and whatever that meant moving forward was ours to define.

Everyone else could shut the hell up.

We were all gathered in Walt's dome, trying to formulate the next plan—hopefully one that provided greater odds of success. I forced my attention back to the conversation, my gaze lingering on the closed door of the medi-pod room.

"He has a harem?" Darby's voice was skeptical. "I thought that was a made-up term."

"I've only heard rumors," Wendra said. "But if they're true, he does."

"I don't think he'll harm the women or children," I said, beginning to pace. "They're too valuable to him."

Daze sat on the floor next to Sampson, doing his best to distract the child. I appreciated that. The kid had been crying off and on, but had seemed to calm down in Daze's presence.

"Since you've heard rumors," Lockland said, "do you know where his base is located? Considering how the militia headquarters were protected, we have to assume his personal area will be even more so."

"Look, all I know," Wendra said, "is that this Tillman guy is a sadist and a murderer. The militia up north has been trying to recruit our tribe for years, but we resisted. My sustainee brother Lucas fell in with them, but escaped a few years later. He had a horrible experience. Then, when they came this time, they said they'd kill us all if he didn't cooperate, and we believed them. They took Freedom's wives, Lea and Mimi, and all the children, which was the only reason Freedom agreed to help. He didn't join up earlier—not because he was against helping Tillman, but because he was a lazy bastard. When they took his kids, he had no choice. He loved them in his own way. I guess."

Helena made a noise in the back of her throat, but chose not to comment further on Freedom. Instead, she said, "We must do everything we can to get Lea, Mimi, and the children back."

I nodded. "We will."

"I saw the look in his eye," Bender said. "Tillman and I share a lot of the same traits, except for the sadist and murderer parts. If we go in there, he'll blow us all up rather than surrender."

"Then we'll blow him up first," Lockland said.

"Not without harming those kids," Bender said. "He knows that. That's why he took them."

I glanced over at the heap in the corner that was Albert.

The man had been gravely injured, but he wasn't

dead yet. Walt sat next to him, because Walt was a nice guy. I'd wanted to give him Babble immediately, but Walt argued it would've been useless. If Albert was still alive by the time Case got out of the medi-pod, we were going to put him in and see what happened.

"When we were flying toward the militia headquarters," I said to Maisie, who was sitting in a chair against the wall, "did you happen to sense anything else in the immediate vicinity? Any radio signals that weren't associated with the towers?"

She shook her head. "No. But I did scan Tillman's craft before he got out of range, and I found a location marker."

"What was the location?" I asked.

"The cave where you found the Eye Diffs," she answered.

My eyebrows rose. "He had the cave's location logged into his craft?"

"Yes."

"Was it set as his current destination in his flight recorder?" I asked. "As in, is he heading there now? Or did he just come from there?"

"Neither. His craft is equipped with a directional keeper, which was standard for the X class. It was the only location entered."

I continued to pace. "I'm not sure he would go there now, but it might be a good idea to check the area out soon. See why he has that particular location entered and nothing else."

"If we can fly in close enough," Bender added, "Maisie can detect if he's there, so we're not going in cold. If he's absent, we investigate."

"I can't believe he got away," I grumbled, crossing my arms.

"We came up with that plan in an hour," Lockland said. "It was the best we had on short notice. Maisie only gave it a thirty-eight percent chance of success. We did what we had to do. It didn't work the way we planned, but this is not a total loss. We didn't sacrifice anyone, and Tillman has been further depleted."

Nobody had brought up the fact that Maisie had controlled Julian during the confrontation. I was going to leave that alone for the time being. It was sad that we'd lost Matteo, as having an extra LiveBot, even in retail mode, would've been an advantage. But Lockland was right. No one had died, and I was happy he'd been our only casualty.

Except Case, who was being fixed right now.

I glanced toward the small room, agitation manipulating my thought process. Being forced to wait grated on my every nerve. "It's almost blackout, and we're all exhausted," I said. "I say we get some sleep and finish this in the morning. There's a spare dome and a couple of vacant buildings, so everyone has a place to go. Let's transport people, and we can come up with a plan when we're all fully awake and recharged."

"Sounds good," Lockland said, looking as beat as the rest of us.

I glanced at Knox, who had a mild headache and a lump at his temple, but had otherwise maintained he was fine. "You're in charge of transport. You know which places are best."

Knox stood, nodding. "We have plenty of beds. I'll take the women and children." Wendra and Helena joined him by the stairs. Sampson was reluctant to leave Daze. The small boy whimpered as Helena tugged him along.

I walked over, leaning down to whisper in Daze's ear, "Why don't you go with him? Helena will appreciate your company, and you can help keep watch over them." I drew out my HydroSol and handed it to him.

His eyes widened as he took it. "I can go, but what about you?"

"I'll stay here with Walt and Case and make sure Case stays in that medi-pod as long as he needs to, which you know will take effort on my part because he's so stubborn." I smiled. The kid's concern was endearing. "We'll be fine."

Helena placed her hand on Sampson's shoulder, comforting the boy. "We would appreciate your company, Daze. I'm certain Sampson would sleep better with you near."

Sampson nodded, his tousled hair bobbing as a single tear leaked down his cheek. Helena had shielded the boy from most of the violence in the end, but I hoped knowing his father had been killed, even in self-defense, wouldn't leave a lasting impression on him. I'd witnessed Freedom's abuse of Sampson. He was better off without his dad, but that kind of stuff would be addressed later in his life.

Darby moved forward. "I'll go, too. There's not enough room here anyway. I'd also like to check on the rest of the tribe. Make sure everyone is calm and comfortable."

I nodded. "That's a good idea." I glanced over at Lockland and Bender. "Darby's right. There aren't enough beds here. One of you stay with Albert, but the others should go and get some rest."

"I'll stay," Bender offered.

Lockland stood. "I'll go with Darby and check on everyone. I want to talk to the people in the tribe and see if anyone has any information about Tillman and his group."

"Take Julian," I offered. "We'll keep Maisie. She can stand guard outside. Meet back here at dawn."

Darby gestured to Julian, and the retail bot followed him without question.

Once everyone was gone and Maisie was positioned in front of the dome, I met Bender's gaze from across the room.

He was grinning like a fiend.

Great, here we go.

"Don't start," I said. "I'm not in the mood."

"What?" Bender shrugged innocently. "I can't comment on witnessing you finally profess your love after all these years?"

"Years? It's been a few weeks. And I didn't *profess*

anything. It was a kiss, nothing more. I was relieved he was alive. We were celebrating."

"It was a lot of kisses. Like, tons. So many we couldn't see your face for ten minutes straight."

I shot him an irritated look and sat down, resting my elbows on my thighs, one hand winding behind my neck. "I don't give a shit if it was fifty million kisses. I didn't profess anything. I was glad he was okay. We're together. Get used to it."

"Together, huh? Like in a *relationship*?"

"No." I hesitated. Were we? Too soon to tell. "I don't know. Maybe. Whatever it is—it's not any of your damn business."

"A man is entitled to his curiosity. It's unlike you to show this much affection for anything. Thus, people mistaking you for a LiveBot."

"That happened *one* time. It's like me. Get over it. Or I'll facilitate your journey with a strategically placed boot kick to the head." I had perfected, better than Bender, what we referred to as The Bender. I was lighter and more flexible. It knocked most people out on the first try, and it hurt like a bitch.

Bender raised his hands, still grinning, showing teeth. "I'm over it."

"Good. Then this should be the last time it ever comes up."

Bender tipped his head back and laughed. It was a deep, gurgling chortle. "Like hell."

Chapter 20

When the medi-pod beeped, I sprang off the ground, startled. I'd been asleep next to it. Walt had given me a thin blanket and a pillow, but they hadn't facilitated any real comfort. The door to the room was closed, and it was dark. I flipped on my shoulder light, and a blue glow glinted off the pod. I hadn't checked my timepiece when Case went in, but he'd been in there for at least three hours.

For such a seemingly small injury, it seemed to take a long time to partially heal.

I pressed the release button and opened the lid.

Case was asleep, his face serene. He looked so peaceful, I didn't want to wake him. If Albert was still alive, he was slated to go in next. But in this very moment, I didn't give a shit about Albert.

As I gazed down at the man who'd stumbled into my life completely unexpectedly, I felt at peace.

Actually, I had no idea if it was peace, but whatever it was, it was welcome.

This outskirt—this mystery of a man—had managed to find some opening into my soul I'd had no idea was there.

Case's eyes fluttered open. "Hello," he whispered, his voice cracking.

"Hi, yourself," I said. "How do you feel?"

He rubbed his side where the wound had been. "Mended."

"Mended, as in fully healed? Or mended, as in you need a pain blocker from Walt?"

"Mended, as in good enough," he answered as he began to pull himself up. His black T-shirt stretched across his chest as his eyes found mine.

We met in the middle, our lips rushing together as his hands tracked through my hair. He held on tightly, like he thought he might lose me if he let go. After a moment, I broke the kiss, murmuring, "I'm glad you're okay."

"Me, too," he breathed, his forehead resting against mine, his hands cradling my face. "If I wasn't, I wouldn't have had a chance to experience this."

Reluctantly, I stepped back as he emerged from the medi-pod. Once he was out, his arms locked around me. Then my back was against the wall, his lips on my neck. I'd never experienced anything so incredible. My fingers dug into his shoulders as I clung to him, wanting to explore every inch of him, a small moan issuing out of my throat.

A knock sounded on the door.

"This bastard is still alive," Bender called. "I need to get him in there."

Case and I broke apart, both of us panting.

"Okay, bring him in," I said, running my hands through my hair, trying to compose myself.

Case reached over and opened the door.

Bender ignored us as he carried Albert to the medi-pod, Walt following. "He hasn't got much left in him," Walt chattered. "We must put this on the highest setting. It will likely take the rest of the night."

"I'll stay in here with him," Bender said.

Case reached down without a word and plucked up the blanket and pillow from the ground, and grabbing my hand, he led me out of the room.

I went eagerly.

The outskirt walked directly over to the hatch and pulled it open. We descended the steps, the door closing behind us. It was dark, save for my blue light, but we didn't need any more than that.

Case spread the blanket on the ground. Seconds later, his mouth was back on mine.

Waves of emotion crashed through me as I tried to grapple with the intensity of what I was experiencing. Case tugged his shirt over his head, reaching for my vest. I already had the zipper down, so it slipped off easily. "Set it down gently," I murmured, my teeth tugging at his bottom lip. "There's stuff in there that can explode."

He smiled. "I know." His eyes were like two pools of

hot mercury, laden with intent. The way he looked at me, desired me, wanted me, sent my senses into overdrive.

He took his time undressing me, his lips lingering everywhere, leaving a heated trail down my body. His fingertips skimmed my sides and my breasts, forcing them into tight peaks and sending chills up my spine over and over again.

When I couldn't stand it any longer—our breathing ragged and raspy—he guided me gently down to the blanket. I took his weight eagerly, my hips arching in invitation. In a tangle of arms and legs, both of us holding on for life, the crescendo built immediately, matching our frantic pace.

It was both gentle and hard, soft and rough, coupled by our intense need for each other.

Crying out, my face buried in his neck, my hands gripping him tightly, I lost myself. I'd lain with only one other in my lifetime, but that had been nothing like this.

A cascade of emotions rippled through me as my release came, spinning me out of control. My head lolled from side to side, my eyes squeezed shut, and my heart raced like it would explode out of my chest.

I'd never, in my entire life, felt this alive.

~

I woke up in pain. Not from our lovemaking, which hadn't stopped until we'd both been fully satiated, but from my injuries. I was currently—and contentedly, if I discounted the pain—intertwined with Case, who was snoring lightly. I didn't want to wake him, but getting my aches under control was a top priority. I'd administered the darts in my vest pocket before I'd gone to sleep next to the medi-pod. But it'd been too many hours since my last round.

I eased myself up slowly, locating my vest, which was off to the side, the blue light at the shoulder muted, but enough to see by. Very gently, I extracted myself from the man sleeping beside me. Crawling a few paces, I found the rest of my clothing, slipping on my pants, cringing as the movement exacerbated the pain in my leg and hip, not allowing myself to call out and wake up the outskirt.

My shirt went next, but I left the rest, making my way up the stairs in bare feet. I opened the hatch as quietly as I could, relieved to see three darts waiting for me on the ground. Leave it to Walt to think of everything.

I shut the hatch and scooped them up. The medi-pod whirred softly from behind the closed door. I padded over and entered the room. Bender sat on a chair next to the wall, arms crossed, head down. He had his shoulder light on, so it wasn't pitch dark.

As I came in, he raised his head, giving me a short nod.

I pulled up a chair, the only other one in the room, and sat, plunging all three darts into my thigh at once, resting against the wall, exhaling as the pain began to recede. "I'm going to kiss Walt the next time I see him."

Bender snorted softly. "Damn, you're terrible with darts." He rearranged his body, stretching his legs out in front of him as he massaged his arms. He was way too big for that chair. "Honestly, they don't need to go in that far. They're designed to release their contents at the slightest contact with bodily fluid. Now they're imbedded in your leg." He made a face.

I plucked the darts out without issue and set them on the floor next to me. "I didn't know you were such a baby about needles," I said, settling back in my seat, happy the pain was all but gone. "I like to get them in as fast as possible. It's the same if you poke a little or a lot."

"I'm no baby," Bender countered. "And it's *not* the same. Two millimeters versus twenty is a big difference."

I chuckled. "I'll keep that in mind."

"How's Case?"

"Sleeping."

We were both quiet for a few minutes, the sound of the medi-pod oddly soothing. "So, you and Case got together, huh?" he said.

"Yep," I replied, not moving my head from its comfortable position against the wall.

"It's a done deal."

"I thought we weren't going to talk about this again."

Ignoring me, Bender replied in a tired voice, "For what it's worth, I think it's a good thing."

"Thanks."

"Anytime." After a few minutes, he added, "If you need any advice, I'm available."

I made a choking sound. "Yeah, because you're so adept in the relationship department? I've never even seen a woman near you besides Claire."

"I'm adept."

"Nice to hear. Does this mean we can stop talking about this?"

"Not in the least."

I chuckled, then changed the subject. "How long has Albert been in there?"

"I don't know. I've been in and out of sleep. A few hours maybe?"

"Do you think he'll heal up enough to talk?"

Bender grunted. "He might not die, but I don't think he'll be in much shape to answer our questions. It's a miracle he's still breathing. He must've been a stubborn son of a bitch in his previous life."

Albert had been hit in multiple places by Bender's Web laser, which had seared lines right through his body. The fact he hadn't bled out before we got him into the pod was stunning.

I bent forward, bracing my head in my hands, exhaustion washing over me. "I can't believe all this stuff has happened. We went from living our own lives, salvaging, and getting by, to a possible apocalypse, mass extermination, and a war with the militia we had no idea about, all in a matter of weeks." I dropped my arms, glancing up wearily. "Now I have a kid and a partner. We've discovered science that we had no idea was even possible to re-create. We found a way to cure seekers, make decent food, and control pain better." I laid my head back, rocking it against the bumpy wall as I idly shook it from side to side. "It seems like the only logical explanation would be for us to wake up and discover this was all a dream."

"I hear you," Bender said. "It's been a wild ride, one I didn't see coming at all. That's what bothers me the most. To find out a militia this big has had an agenda in place for all these years is a fucking travesty. That our government has been compromised, and we had no idea about it, is insane. Stuff like that makes me crazy."

I glanced at him, my position unmoving. "We have to stop Tillman. Whatever it takes."

"We will."

"It's going to come at a cost," I said. We weren't going to emerge from this unscathed.

"I know."

Rustling outside the room preceded Walt shuffling in. "How's the patient?" he asked as he made his way to the medi-pod.

"He hasn't made a sound," Bender said. "There's a possibility he died in there."

"Oh, I don't think so," Walt said. "If there's anything this old medi-pod is good at, it's staving off death."

As Walt inspected the patient through the small cutout on top, I got up and exited the room. Surprisingly, I found Case on the floor of the main room, back up against the wall, fully dressed.

I sat down next to him. "How do you feel?"

"Emotionally or physically?" He flashed me a smile. It wasn't anywhere near his usual stoic expression.

I liked it. He most certainly had a dimple.

"Physically." I wasn't ready to jump into anything remotely concerning feelings. "In need of some of Walt's pain blockers?" He nodded, and I got up to get some from the table, where Walt had left a stack, bless his old, stony heart. I brought three back, the same colors Walt had given me. "Do you want me to do it? Or do you want to? Full disclosure, Bender thinks I suck at this."

"I trust you."

I cradled his forearm in my lap and decided to administer these gently. I pricked the blue dart just under the skin, and like magic, the contents emptied into Case's vein. I did the next two, and when I was finished, Case leaned his head back, sighing. "Thank you."

"You're welcome."

Case arched his shoulder, and I slid in beside him, resting my head in the crook of his neck. He gripped my side possessively, his hand warm. "Life is going to be hard until we settle this thing with Tillman," I said.

"*Um hm,*" he murmured.

"After that, maybe life will go back to normal." I made a noise in the back of my throat, a mix between a snort and a laugh. "What am I talking about? There won't be any normal. Everything is strange and weird."

"I'll take that over normal," he replied.

"You know, us being in a relationship makes things more complicated."

"No, it simplifies them."

He might be right. "I'm not going to change into something different now that we're together."

"Why would you?"

"Just checking."

He chuckled.

Walt emerged from the medi-pod room. "He's awake. I fear he doesn't have much time left, so if you're going to interrogate him, it needs to be done immediately. Let me get the Babble."

Case was the first to get up. He extended his arm to me. I grabbed on, and he hauled me up, his hand landing firmly around my waist as we walked into the medi-pod room.

Chapter 21

To say Albert was in bad shape was gross understatement. He was alive, but only out of sheer tenacity on his part. It was clear he'd been stubborn his entire life. Bender had lifted him out of the medi-pod and managed to prop him up in a chair, using a blanket and several scraps of fabric to strap him in without further exacerbating his injuries. We were trying our best to be kind.

The medi-pod had glued some of his wounds together, but that was about it.

The Babble had relaxed him, but his breathing was labored. It gave me no pleasure to interrogate him like this, but it was necessary for the fate of the city. I held that close. "Albert, I need you to focus," I instructed from my seat in front of him. Maisie stood behind me, Case leaned up against the wall, and Bender sat in a chair beside me. Walt had opted not to participate. I didn't blame him. "Who else survived the blasts at the headquarters?"

"Only a few of us survived," he moaned deliriously. "So many explosions. The building rained down upon our heads."

"Do you know where Tillman's personal headquarters are located?" Bender asked.

"He's a private man, Tillman," Albert mumbled. "Never takes orders. Thinks he's in charge."

I raised a single eyebrow, glancing at Bender. "No surprise there."

"Who's in charge of your operation?" Bender asked.

"I am," Albert stated. "I must succeed. This has to work."

"Why does this have to work?" I asked, sensing the urgency in his voice. I wasn't exactly sure what *this* was, but it was clear he was worried about something.

"If it doesn't work, they'll kill me. I know they will," he said, moaning again, his head dropping forward.

"Who will kill you?" Case asked, coming to stand next to Maisie behind me.

"The man Tillman protects," he answered mysteriously, his head still bowed.

"Who is Tillman protecting?" I asked, turning to Bender. "If he says Brock Shannon, we'll know he's hallucinating."

Brock Shannon, we'd learned from Reed, had either put this entire movement together many years ago, or he was the personality used to motivate others to join the cause. Either way, the man had to be dead. He would be much too old now to have survived all these years.

"Brock Shannon."

I threw up my hands and stood. "I've had it with these guys and their reverence for Brock Shannon."

Case took my place, grabbing the chair and turning it so he could straddle it. "Albert, do you believe Brock Shannon is alive?"

The man wheezed before answering, "Of course he's alive."

"How old is he?" Bender asked.

"No one knows," Albert replied.

"My guess is that Tillman has been orchestrating this for years," I said. Trying to pace in the small confines of the room wasn't optimal. "Maybe Tillman was tasked with protecting an aging Brock Shannon in the beginning, and once he died, they decided to keep his spirit alive to make sure everyone stayed in line."

"That makes sense," Bender said. "But we're not going to find out what really went down until we hear it straight from Tillman or locate a trail."

"Albert doesn't seem like a man who's feared much during his lifetime," Case said. "He carried himself with complete self-assurance, right up to the end, and he didn't hesitate to shoot Wendra. But he has a healthy fear of Brock. There has to be a reason for that."

"Have you ever met Brock Shannon?" Bender asked Albert.

"Once," Albert said.

I came to a stop. "When did you meet him?"

"Fifteen years ago," Albert replied, "when he started the medi-pod program."

"The medi-pods designed to cure seekers?" I asked.

"Yes," Albert replied. "He ordered us to round up the scientists and engineers."

"Then what happened?" Case asked.

"He was very old," Albert said. "He had a partner. A very smart man. He was put in charge of overseeing the program."

I nodded along in spite of myself. We'd already heard a version of this from Reed. There had apparently been a wealthy benefactor, which was likely the partner Albert was referring to. And when he died, the program died with him. "Once this man was gone, you decided to kill off the scientists and engineers so they wouldn't speak about the lifesaving program."

"Yes," Albert agreed, his breath coming in short gasps, his torso bending forward. "We couldn't afford…to keep inferior human beings. It was against our new code."

"Who decided on this new code?" I asked. To the guys, I said, "He better not say Brock Shannon."

"Brock Shannon."

I gritted my teeth. These people were certifiable.

"It doesn't really matter," Bender said. "We need to find Tillman and end this. It's a simple equation."

"You know where Tillman is?" Case asked.

"The man is a mystery," Albert said.

"Do you have plans to go back to the city?" I asked.

"We will defeat the infiltrators," Albert murmured. "Then the city will be ours."

That wasn't going to happen, but there was no need to tell Albert he wasn't going to be there to see it.

Walt entered the room carrying a fistful of pain blockers. "I think this man has done enough. Let's put him back in the medi-pod."

I nodded. "It's pretty clear Albert doesn't know much about what was going on down South. He thought he was calling the shots, but it has to be Tillman."

Case, Maisie, and I left the room as Walt and Bender lifted Albert back into the medi-pod. I had no idea if the man would survive, but I was okay with our interrogation. It had been necessary, even though we hadn't gleaned as much information as I'd hoped for.

Bender and Walt emerged a moment later. "We still have a few hours until dawn," Bender said. "Let's get some sleep. We can leave Maisie in charge of Albert."

"Okay, sounds good. We regroup at dawn," I said.

Without comment, Case took my hand and led me down the stairs.

~

"And that's all you got from him?" Lockland asked.

Lockland had gotten here with Julian at first light. Darby and Daze and the others hadn't arrived yet.

"Yes," I said. "Albert was in bad shape, and we were exhausted. But I'm certain he didn't know that much about Tillman. Albert might've been heading things at the city level, but not so much inside the organization. Or he would've known more."

Albert hadn't survived the night, even though Walt had kept a close eye on him and had even given him some amino boosters.

"As I see it," Lockland said, "we have two choices. We can head back to the city and prepare for battle, or we can go after Tillman immediately and try to finish this before he has a chance to regroup."

"I don't see many advantages to going back to the city," I said. "If Tillman attacked us there, it would be messy and would involve a lot of innocent people."

"I agree," Lockland said. "But at this point, Tillman and his group are depleted, and it may take them years to gather enough resources to come after us. During that time, we could build a big enough resistance and have a lot of firepower in place."

"No, Holly's right. We end this now," Bender said. "We can't have this hanging over us for years, never knowing when the strike will come. It would affect all the progress we want to make, like taking the scientists back to the city and having them create something with their resources. Word would get out about the changes, and as soon as it did, it would trickle down to Tillman and his group. Then we'd have even more to lose."

I sat by one of Walt's tables, this one filled with vials. I picked up a glass tube and rolled it between my fingers. "We go after him now," I said, my voice filled with determination. "We can't forget about Lea and

Mimi and the children. We promised Helena we would get them back. Their lives are just as valuable as everyone else's."

"I say we start with the cave," Case added. "It had to be programmed into his craft for a reason. Maisie might be able to pick up on his whereabouts if he's close by, or if he's been there recently. It's as good of a place to start as any. I'm sure there'll be clues to find."

I was about to ask Maisie about our chances of defeating Tillman if we found him immediately, with only four men, when the door to the dome banged open and Knox and Darby rushed in.

Knox was out of breath by the time he reached the bottom of the steps. "The tribespeople have disappeared."

I stood. "What are you talking about? Disappeared where?"

"I have no idea. They took the extra crafts and…just left."

"Did they take the children?" I asked.

"Yes, they're all gone," he answered. "I did rounds this morning. No one was home."

"What about Elond and Nareen?" Lockland asked.

"I didn't check," Knox said. "The scientists live outside the main boundary. But if I had my guess, I'd say they're gone, too."

My gaze landed solidly on Walt.

The old man had his back to us, busying himself with the bio-printer and a vat of slurry. He was making us a meal. Crossing my arms, I eased up behind him. "Care to explain?" I asked. "Don't bother telling us you don't know anything about it. Elond and Nareen wouldn't go anywhere without telling you."

He turned slowly, his bushy eyebrows furrowed, the container still in his hand, brown liquid sloshing around. "They left with my blessing. It's not safe here anymore. You were going to move them up to the city anyway, so in essence, they're just getting a head start." He shrugged like it was no big deal that the entire tribe had deserted the area.

I dropped my arms, frustrated. "Why didn't you tell us? We could've *helped.*"

"We couldn't risk it," he said. "If you disagreed with our plan, you would've tried to stop us and likely would've been successful."

"Where are they going?" I asked. "They don't know the city. What Elond and Nareen have is too valuable to risk. It was a mistake not to tell us. We could've provided protection."

"Those two have been packing up their supplies since you left the first time," Walt said. "They were ready to leave at a moment's notice. You're forgetting that we all came from the city. It's been many years, but we worked out of several laboratories. One of those locations should suffice until the rest of us arrive."

"Did they take all the crafts we had from Tillman and his men?" I asked. There were eleven crafts in total—four from my crash site and seven from our recent altercation.

"They took six," Walt answered. "We couldn't pass

up the opportunity. Crafts have been scarce in this area for a very long time. We believe you are here to help us and that your intentions are honorable." His expression was earnest. "But you're not one of us, and we have to look out for our own. We saw an opportunity, so we took it. You cannot fault us for that."

Lockland stood next to me. "We understand why you did it," he said. "But Holly's right. You should've told us. We could've provided a safer refuge for them and, at minimum, made sure they arrived in the city unharmed."

Knox was visibly hurt, slowly shaking his head. "I can't believe you didn't tell me. I'm a part of this tribe. I deserved to know."

Walt rested his hand on Knox's shoulder. "Son, you're proving to be a very astute leader, and I'm thoroughly impressed. What you've accomplished in a short amount of time, such as organizing things and keeping us safe, has been very encouraging. But you've put your faith in these people here." He used the slurry bucket to gesture toward us. "It would've weighed too heavily on you not to say anything, and I couldn't put you in that position. But in the future, you will be apprised of all of our decisions. I give you my solemn word."

"My sister, Helena, and Sampson are still here, right?" Case asked.

"Yes, they're still here," Walt answered, shuffling back to the table. "But there's a craft waiting if you decide to take them to safety. A battleground is no place for women and children."

"Walt, I'm going to pretend you didn't just say that," I said. "But I understand and agree with you. There's no need for Wendra, Helena, and Sampson to be here for what comes next." I glanced at Darby. "Are you ready to go home? You and Daze can fly the women back to the city and oversee the tribe, make sure everyone stays safe and has a place to sleep. You can set up Elond and Nareen in Tandor's old lab until we make the Emporium safe again." The militia had sent spies and rigged bombs there. We'd have to clean the place out first and make sure there weren't any surprises waiting for us.

A mixture of eagerness and hesitation crossed Darby's features. "Are you sure you want me to go back? Don't you need us here?"

"No," I answered. "The seven of us will be enough. We'll keep Julian, but you guys should go back. Keep a low profile once you enter the city. Make sure you don't announce your presence. Don't even tell Claire. If all goes well down here, we should only be a day or two behind you."

"What about Walt?" Darby asked, gesturing to the old man. "He can't stay here by himself."

Walt chuckled. "I can defend myself just fine. I have a lot of precautions in place, and I still have some packing up to do. As you can see, I move slowly these days."

I didn't love the idea of leaving Walt here alone, but

once we took care of the threat, we could pick up Walt and some of his supplies with the mover drone. It would take multiple trips to get everything transferred. "Walt, do you know how to fly a craft?" I asked. "We'll leave one behind for you in the event of an emergency."

"I think I could manage," Walt said. "It's been many years, but I was a fairly decent pilot in my day."

"It's settled, then," I said. "Now we have to figure out how to finish Tillman and be done with this."

Chapter 22

"The cave is up ahead," Maisie said. "Twenty-three kilometers northwest."

"I can't imagine he's holed up there, biding his time," I said. "Just waiting around for us to arrive."

Case was flying, I was in the passenger seat, and Maisie sat in the back. Behind us, Lockland flew a craft with Bender in front, Knox and Julian in back. After much discussion, we'd decided to leave the mover drone with Walt. We would be less conspicuous that way. If Walt couldn't fly it, he had two other crafts to choose from, though one had been badly damaged in the shootout with Tillman.

"I don't think he's there," Case said. "But we could find something of value. Something that might explain what's going on. If both Dixon and Tillman knew about this place, it has to mean something."

I shifted in my seat. "Maisie, are there any humans nearby?"

"There are no unknown humans or crafts in the area."

"This cave must be important," I said. "After all, we found the Eye Diffs here, so Roman either stashed them here himself, or he gave them to someone to take them there for safekeeping. With Dixon, that's three different pieces to this story, three men who are somehow connected. Dixon used to be involved in the Bureau of Truth, so it makes sense he would know Tillman. But what about Roman? Where does he fit in?"

"I don't know," Case said. "It's definitely not a coincidence."

I nodded. "Agreed. It feels like people on the same team might've been working against each other. Albert and the Bureau of Truth against Tillman and Dixon, or Tillman and Brock's partner, whoever that was. Tillman used Freedom to get to you. He kidnapped your brother's family and your sister, knowing it would be a trigger for you. My guess is he got that information from Dixon. But why?"

Case was quiet. "I think you're right. It has something to do with me. Tillman wants me to come after him. But it doesn't make any sense. Dixon and I had a…tumultuous relationship at best. We weren't close. He gave orders, and for the most part, I followed them. We got along like I imagine an employer would treat an employee. But I always wondered why he chose me. Before he killed off the militia I was in, we hadn't spoken more than a few words to each other. I've always thought it was strange that he kept me alive."

Maisie interrupted, "The cave is just up ahead. I advise parking in the same area you did before. It's the only stable ground nearby."

I thought about what Case had told me. "You said your parents both died when you were young. Do you know that for a fact?"

Case shrugged. "It's a blur. I didn't see them die, but suddenly I was living with the elderly couple I told you about. I was too young to question it."

"You said the older couple kept you indoors. That they were really protective of you. It wasn't until you were seven years old that you broke out."

"That's true," Case said. "The old man died, and the woman didn't have the heart to keep me locked up any longer. I ran away immediately."

"What if they were your grandparents or something?" I asked. "Did anybody ever come to visit?"

"There was one man. He came by a few times. It's a little hazy. I think they called him Morty." Case dropped altitude quickly, setting us down in the clearing that led to the cave entrance.

"It all has to be connected." My tone was adamant. "Tillman was happy when he saw you in those last few minutes. His eyes were locked on you the entire time. Dixon took you for a reason. He was involved with the Bureau of Truth and had meetings regularly with people he kept secret from you. They must've all been in the know." Beside us, Lockland set his craft down. Everyone got out.

Case and I led the way to the cave.

"This place is in the middle of nowhere," Bender said. "But anything out of the city feels like the middle of nowhere, so I guess it's all the same."

At the cave entrance, I announced, "Case and I think this might be connected to him and his past. Once we get in there, we go through everything. We need to uncover any clues we can find connecting Dixon, Tillman, and Roman. We leave nothing unturned."

After two hours of work, we'd uncovered exactly zero information.

Maisie was an asset. She scanned the boxes before we even tried to open them, deeming the contents worth our time or not. Even with her help, we were coming up empty.

"There's nothing here," Bender grumbled. He and I were in the back room, going through the containers with the Bliss Corp logo that had contained the Eye Diffs. "There's nothing connected to anyone, much less Dixon, Tillman, Roman, or someone named Morty."

"Keep looking. There has to be something." I turned in a slow circle. "We're just not searching in the right place yet." I wandered back into the main area and paused by the box of guns that Daze had gone through not too long ago. It was stacked with a bunch of other stuff against the wall. I got down on my knees and shifted some boxes out of the way. The wall behind them began to crumble, just a little at first, but then I began to dig. More rock fell away.

"I think I found a tunnel!"

The others joined me.

"Maisie, what's behind there?" Lockland asked.

"All I detect is rock and a pocket of air," she said.

The entrance to the tunnel had been filled with loose stones. Something was located behind this, there was no question. "Can you see what's beyond here?" I asked Maisie. "According to the diameter of this hole, this tunnel entrance is only a meter high. Only large enough to crawl through. Check the entire room for more hidden features." Case and Bender joined me in moving rocks. Julian and Lockland began to tug boxes away from the wall.

Maisie turned, gesturing left. "There. I didn't catch it before, because the wall is thick and the interior mimics this space, but there is a pocket of air, and within it, man-made features, such as furniture and some technology."

"The tunnel must twist around that way," I said. It took us thirty minutes to clear the debris, exposing a hole big enough to crawl through. "They went to a lot of trouble to cover this up." My heart beat faster as I sat back up on my knees, glancing at Case. "I think you should go in first. Whatever we find in that room is going to be important."

Case nodded as he switched on both his shoulder lights. He entered the tunnel, I followed, then Maisie, Bender, and Lockland. I heard Lockland say, "Julian, stay here. Keep watch. If you hear or see anything, let us know."

Julian replied with a jaunty, "Will do! Happy to be of service."

The tunnel immediately turned left, as predicted.

The air was stale inside. We crawled for a while, then took another left. The tunnel walls were too smooth to have been formed naturally. "Whoever excavated this used some sort of heavy machinery," I said.

The tunnel finally connected us to a fairly large room. Case emerged first, turning to help me up. I stood, brushing off my pants. Once all of us had piled into the space, we glanced around.

It was filled with old computers and monitors, hooked up like they were waiting for their owner to return. The technology in here was so antiquated, I'd seen only a few of these boxy components before.

I walked over to a monitor and ran my finger along the top. Rock dust a centimeter thick tumbled off. There was a sound behind me as Lockland flicked a switch. A generator jumped to life, the motor revving like a small turbine engine. "There's power," Lockland said. "This generator has been retrofitted with a state-of-the-art battery."

Bender took a seat in front of one of the computers. "The technology in here is at least seventy-five years old, premeteor blast."

I glanced at Maisie. "Can you tell us what we're looking at?"

Maisie took a seat next to Bender, her fingers automatically hitting the keyboard in front of her, punching in letters and numbers rapidly.

The monitor in front of her sprang to life, files

popping up on the screen. "None of this is AI-compatible technology," she replied. "Bender is correct. These are old units meant for processing and keeping data files only. They were revered by some, as hackers couldn't infiltrate their systems from the outside. They were not connected to the world's mass network, because the engineers of these models had reverted back to basic data language. The passcodes will be easy to break. Just give me a moment."

We all waited anxiously for her to get inside the system.

I made my way over to a crude shelving unit and picked up some old papers lying on top of it. They were brittle and yellowed, too faded to read, but had the Bliss Corp logo emblazoned across the top. "This all has to do with Bliss Corp," I said. "They're behind whatever this place is."

"I've located personal user files," Maisie said. "There is one starred as important." Maisie began to read from a document on the screen. "'My name is Martin S. Bancroft, entrepreneur and owner of Bliss Corp. They have informed me there will be a catastrophic event in approximately eighteen months. In preparation, I have acquired a safe refuge to prepare for the worst. I've purchased land—a mountaintop, actually—in which I will carve out a space to keep all of my pertinent data stored and secured. The powers that be have elected not to inform the masses and are actively trying to prevent the forthcoming apocalypse. But the scientists in my employ who have been informed tell me it will be nearly impossible to derail what's headed our way, as it's far too big to be averted. It will take nothing short of a miracle of epic proportions to save the world as we know it.'"

The information was staggering.

My hand settled over my quaking heart. The elite had known about the meteor strike—*for eighteen months.* They'd been given time to prepare. But nobody had bothered to tell the rest of the population.

I knew this to be true, as there was no public record of previous knowledge about the meteor—by anyone. But the elite had known, and they'd managed to keep it a secret.

Case clasped my hand as Maisie continued reading.

"'The new Plush strain hasn't worked as well as we'd hoped. It's causing unforeseen complications, but that may be a good thing, as the survivors of the apocalypse, if there are any, might be grateful to be lost in pleasure, rather than live in torment. For now, we have decided to keep it on the market.'"

I gasped.

Maisie kept going. "'I'm making arrangements for my wife and two sons to have accommodations underground. I'm in the process of building a bunker down South, which the contractors have assured me can withstand a strike of great magnitude. The scientists tell me that, if the projected trajectory is correct, there will be a thin area along the East Coast that has a good chance of surviving. I will stay within that zone.'"

I couldn't hold it any longer. I was furious. "They knew!" I exclaimed as my boot came down, sending a cloud of rock dust billowing up. "Those bastards *knew.* Down to the approximate area where the strikes would land. They were monitoring the trajectory, so they knew it would collide with the moon first. And they intentionally kept the bad Plush going, because he thought it would help the survivors cope." It was all beyond shocking.

Lockland pulled out a chair and sat with a thump. "Maisie," he said, "keep reading. We need the rest of the story."

Maisie continued, "'To ensure that my wife, Chandra, and my two sons, Martin Jr. and Robert, have all the resources they need to survive, I'm stocking several warehouses around the country with supplies, including weapons, technology, medical supplies, and money. Even though my heart longs to expose this secret to all of those I love, I've been sworn to secrecy. If the scope of this cataclysmic event were to be uncovered, the world would erupt into mass chaos. Instead, I am forced to do this quietly and resourcefully.'"

"Of course there would've been mass chaos," I retorted. "But so many more people would have survived! Instead, you trillionaires and oligarchs prepared for your own survival, so your heirs could live on, while the rest of the people died." I snorted, anger making me vibrate. "So typical from what we know about our ancestors. Greed was the only thing they understood. Those bastards."

"It sounds like this guy did what he said, built a bunker and stocked some warehouses," Bender said. "Who knows if they survived? But he had to have people working for him. There's no way his wife and children could've handled everything on their own."

"Let Maisie finish," Lockland said. "Then maybe we'll have the answers and can go from there. Continue, please."

"'I have made arrangements within the government,'" Maisie continued. "'My children will hold prominent positions if they survive. They will have access to the resources I've left behind to rebuild the city. It's the best I can do. The secret agency will not be revealed until after the strike. Those who swear their allegiance to me will have access to what is mine, on the promise that they will aid my family. I'm signing off with a heavy heart. To all of those who come after me, please know this: I tried my best.'"

I exhaled, which turned into a growl. "The meteor hit sixty years ago. How old do you think the children were at that time?" I asked.

"I'm locating a file that contains photographs," Maisie said. A few seconds later, a picture filled the screen. Two adults and two little boys.

I brought my hand up, cupping it tightly around my mouth so I didn't make a sound.

One of the boys looked exactly like Case.

Chapter 23

Maisie spoke first, breaking the silence. "Cryptic analysis of facial similarities has produced two possible matches within my database. One at ninety-seven percent, the other at sixty-three percent. Facial recognition is an advanced technique that connects genetic commonalities between individuals, but it is highly fallible, as many humans share common traits. DNA testing is required for official determination."

"It's obvious Case is related to this boy," I said, gesturing to the child who resembled him. "They look like brothers. Who's the other match?"

"Daze," Maisie replied.

"Daze?" I gasped. "You're kidding." I bent forward to study the photo. The smaller of the two was blond, like Daze, and I could spot faint similarities, such as the slope of his nose and the rise of his forehead, but nothing I would've picked out without looking closely.

Maisie replied, "After analysis, based on distinct

facial measurements and traits such as eye color and skin color, the conclusion is a likely match to Daze and a more definitive match to Case. But again, genetic testing is required."

Case hadn't said a word.

I turned, settling my hand over his arm, running it lightly up and down. "I know it seems crazy, but we're probably looking at your father when he was a child," I said. "And Daze's father—or possibly grandfather. That means those two kids survived, and you could be Daze's uncle—his real, genetic relative." The entire notion was insane. "If what your presumed grandfather Martin wrote is true, he owned Bliss Corp and set all this up." I scanned the room and the technology covered in dust that had been here for over sixty years.

"Dixon had to have known," Bender said, rubbing the back of his neck with one hand, as shocked as the rest of us. "The Bureau of Truth had to have been the secret society this guy wrote about. They had to have known who Case is. Just look at the photo." Bender gestured at the monitor. "Your likeness to that kid is indisputable. If the Bureau of Truth members, or any of Martin's *faithful* employees, had access to these pictures, they could've identified you."

"We never met Dixon," Lockland said. "But the question is, was he trying to protect you? Or was he using you as a bargaining chip? He killed an entire militia to take you with him. No witnesses left behind. But he shielded you from coming in contact with anyone else. What was his reasoning?"

Case was pale.

"Here," I coaxed, taking his arm. "Sit down for a second." Without argument, he allowed me to lead him to a chair, and once he sat, he placed his head directly in his hands and shook it.

"This doesn't make any sense," he said. "Honestly, I can't believe any of it's true. My parents had nothing. They died with nothing. How could we be connected to any of this?"

I knelt beside him, taking his hand. "Think about what your childhood looked like and what happened after your parents disappeared. The older couple took you in and went to great pains to keep you hidden. Your Sun Optimist family had no idea who you were, but Dixon found you all those years later and wiped out an entire militia to kidnap you. He moved you around regularly. He had secret meetings with people you never saw. By his own admission, he was a former member of the Bureau of Truth. You told us he was the most selfish man you'd ever met. He had to have had an angle. My guess is he was going to trade you for something of value, but whoever was in charge wouldn't meet his demands—or something close to that. It's the only scenario that makes any sense."

Case raised his head. "My parents were simple people with no means. If this was supposed to be my life"—he nodded toward the monitor—"then my grandfather, or whoever he was, didn't achieve his goals."

"There are too many unknowns at this point to draw any real conclusions," I said. "Maybe your father ran away? Maybe he didn't want to be part of the Bureau of Truth once he figured out what they'd evolved into? I don't think Martin expected his secret agency to become a zealot organization. There's so much we don't know, but the pieces are starting to fall together." It was a relief to have some answers, even if they were not the ones we'd hoped for. "There's a big reason we didn't know about the existence of the Bureau of Truth"—I met Bender's and Lockland's gazes—"because it was set up predisaster by a trillionaire who went to great lengths and spent a lot of coin to keep it under wraps. Of course we remained in the dark. He organized resources all over the country and had people working for him before, during, and after the events—until his kids came of age. It's likely the only organization that carried its way through the decimation of our world."

Bender stood, angry. "Tillman knows." His voice was as fierce as I'd ever heard it. "I saw it in that bastard's eyes. He recognized you." He gestured at Case. "He targeted you. He went after your family. We find him, we find the rest of the story. Then we end this. Forever."

Julian shouted something unintelligible.

Maisie's head jerked toward the entrance as she said, "Three crafts are approaching the area."

We made it out of the tunnel in record time.

I brushed myself off in the main room. "If this is Tillman, how did he know we were here?"

"There's a possibility he didn't," Lockland said. "He probably knows what exists here. Maybe he's coming to retrieve it so we don't find it." Lockland's eyes narrowed. "But it's too late for that."

"We have to be ready when he lands," Bender said, heading for the exit. "We confront him here and now. And we do it our way."

As we hurried up the hill, I pulled Maisie and Julian aside, instructing, "Tillman will see our crafts when he approaches. There's no way to conceal the fact we're here. But luckily for us, there's only one place to land, and it's surrounded by a forest of dead trees. Maisie, you go left. Julian, go right. Keep your weapons trained on them. If it looks like they're going to shoot us, make sure you shoot first."

It was the best plan I had. The only plan.

As the LiveBots veered off, going their separate ways, I kept my head down. Once we reached the clearing, the last of the pieces would fall into place. I felt it in my bones. I agreed with Bender. Tillman knew the information we were after. He'd been in on this since birth. If we could get Tillman to talk, which I was certain we would, because he'd proven to be a cocky bastard who would crave the last word, we would finally have our answers.

"Don't pull your weapons out yet, but have them at the ready," Lockland instructed. "We want to send the signal that we want to talk."

The X class craft landed first. Two other crafts landed behind it.

Tillman emerged, barrel-sized thighs and all, grinning, followed by four soldiers with laser guns so large they required shoulder straps and both hands to keep them steady. I'd seen only a few like them in my lifetime. They were military-grade guns from way before the dark days. Tillman certainly didn't lack for firepower.

"I guess it's not surprising to see you here," Tillman said in a tone filled with assurance. This man hadn't lost many battles. But if I had anything to say about it, he'd lose this one. He pinned a greedy gaze on Case. "Dixon bring you here a lot? That fool. He never listened to reason."

This had taken an interesting turn right from the get-go.

Very calmly, Case replied, "What do you know about me and Dixon?"

Tillman cocked his head back and laughed—more like bellowed—rocking up on his toes then back on his heels. "What *don't* I know about you and Dixon? He was my brother once upon a time. Not genetically, of course, because I'm much better-looking. But we were raised together. They sent him up to the city, hoping to put that brain of his to good use. But that shit backfired. He went rogue. Then later, he said he'd found you and wanted to make a trade. Strung us along for years."

"Trade me for what?" Case asked. His voice remained eerily quiet.

"He wanted what was rightfully yours." Tillman chuckled. "Kind of ironic, isn't it? He wanted to be the supreme leader—the captain of the new resistance. He had lots of plans in place. He just needed resources to back them up."

"So, why didn't you accept the trade?" I asked, a challenge in my voice. "Case is the heir, after all, isn't he? Aren't you supposed to protect him? Isn't that what your ancestors signed up for?"

Tillman's gaze landed on me and darkened. "We didn't accept the fucking trade because we don't need him." He jutted his chin toward Case. "After his father left, everything changed." He spat on the ground. "Brock Shannon was a lunatic, and so was his son. Marty took everything we didn't hide when he took off with the Flotilla. After that, our deal was null."

I felt like lofting my hands and shouting, *Wait just a minute!*

Every single thing Tillman had just uttered was completely confusing.

Did he mean that Case's grandfather was Brock Shannon? But we'd just read the missive from a man named Martin Bancroft. Who was who?

"You're going to have to back the hell up," Bender growled. "You know who Case is. How long have you known about him?"

Tillman appeared about to answer, then he smiled. "So, we're going to do this, huh? I'm just going to confess everything I know, and then we'll go about our business of killing each other? I don't think so."

Bender shrugged, his posture indifferent. "You tell us what we want to know, and maybe we'll let you live."

"You're a funny man, Bender," Tillman cracked. "Have you seen the men behind me? There's no chance you're surviving this. We couldn't have met up in a better place. You've got no bombs rigged here, and guess what I have on the way?"

The faint *schick-schick* of propellers sounded in the distance. Small ones. They'd be here soon.

"I have an arsenal of UACs, all laser-equipped," Tillman said. "They're programmed to respond to my commands only. You're outmatched." He looked pleased with himself.

Snorting, and affecting my best haughty tone, I said, "You're using Case's own property against him? Doesn't that go against everything you believe in? I bet your father taught you to be honorable. What happened, Tillman? Did Albert and his crew get to you after all these years?" I had no idea what role Tillman's father might have played in all this, but it had to be connected to some kind of service to Martin Bancroft, or Tillman wouldn't be here.

Fury fluttered over Tillman's features, as I'd predicted it would. Finding the right bait for this man was essential. It seemed I'd located a nerve.

"Albert was a fucking tool!" His voice came out in a roar. "He did everything by the book. He idolized Brock Shannon."

There was a book?

"He handed everything over to Marty," Tillman went on, "except what my father managed to hide. Albert believed all the lies Marty spewed. He was never coming back. Once he left, it was up to us to create the new world order, and now we will finally be able to achieve our mission. That is, once you're gone." He nodded casually toward Case.

I was still fairly lost. We all were.

It was essential to keep Tillman talking. He believed he was going to win this, and that worked in our favor.

Lockland cleared his throat. "So, Brock Shannon was a real person?"

Tillman spat, "Of course he was real. How do you think this got started? It was all him. Him and his crazy ideas, and his fucked-up seeker wife, and his two brats. All this is because of him."

"Are you talking about Martin Bancroft? Is that who Brock Shannon really was?" I asked.

Tillman seethed. "Once upon a time, he might've been Martin Bancroft, but not after the meteor strike. After that, he became Brock Shannon. Always Brock Shannon. He went crazy when his wife was infected with Plush. The rumors were that he'd given it to her himself, trying to calm her down in the days following the disaster. But the asshole had known the end of the world was coming. He'd known. He'd built an empire for his son Marty to run, to ensure that his kin would have it easy while the rest of us were left to rot in this fucking hellscape."

"What about the other one?" Bender asked. "Robert?"

"Robert was smart. The only intelligent one of the bunch. He dedicated his life to trying to cure his freak of a mother. That is, until Marty took off with the Flotilla, leaving Albert in charge. That asshole immediately shut down the program. Seekers were dirty. They were below us. Albert despised Robert. Wanted him wiped from the face of the earth. He was the weak one. The one who would bring us down. In order to do that, he poisoned the whole damn team of scientists. He said it was for Marty. He wanted to keep everything pristine for Marty's return." Tillman shook his head in disgust.

Above us, five small UACs entered the area and hovered ten meters above our heads. They were exact replicas of the one I'd blown out of the sky before I'd crashed. Well, Tillman was right about one thing—we couldn't win in a firefight against them. Their laser shots would be precision perfect.

It was going to take some kind of miracle for us to get out of here alive.

"If Albert wanted everything ready for Marty," Lockland countered, "looking after his son should've been at the top of that list."

Tillman flicked his eyes up at the UACs, grinning like a fiend, his teeth clacking together, before he settled his gaze directly on Case. "That's what Dixon thought, too. But he was dead wrong. Albert hated the mere thought of your existence. We were told you died after your mother fled with a high-ranking official in the organization. He loved her and vowed to keep her away from Marty. When they were finally tracked down, there was no sign of you, so we believed it. But somehow, Dixon got word later that you were still alive. He always had his ear to the ground, spies everywhere. He was ambitious as hell. It took him years, but he found you. He'd been negotiating with us ever since. Wanted to trade you for most of what we had. He was foolish to think Albert would have allegiance to anyone other than Marty, including his son. Then, suddenly, we didn't hear from Dixon anymore. He stopped showing up for our meets." He shrugged. "We figured you killed him. I don't blame you. He had it coming. But what you didn't know is that he'd been hindering our plans to take over the city, following us around, blowing things up unexpectedly. He knew our routes and sabotaged our plans, always staying a little out of reach. He wanted the prize, and he wasn't content to let us have it. So when you killed him, you solved a big problem for us. Thanks for that, buddy."

"Tell me about my uncle Robert"—Case's voice was icy—"while you still have breath left in your body."

Chapter 24

Tillman hesitated for the first time. He felt Case's wrath. We all did. Case's entire life had been a lie. There was no doubt that if Case had been left to run things, taking over from his dad, our city would've been in much better shape now—possibly even thriving.

"I don't have to tell you shit," Tillman said, gesturing at the UACs overhead. "All I have to do is give one command, and they all fire. Then you disappear like you should've all those years ago."

"Tell me about Robert, you asshole," Case demanded, taking a step forward. "He was the only good thing in that family, wasn't he?"

"Yeah, Robert was good, but it didn't make a difference in the end," Tillman spat. "My father tried to help him, tried to convince him that Albert and his crew had it in for him. But when Marty left with the Flotilla, it was over. There was nothing anyone could do."

"Robert had a family," Case said. "A little boy he was forced to leave behind."

Daze. My heart clenched. The kid was going to be shattered to learn this story. If he got the chance to hear it. I was glad Daze was safe. That was the only good thing about this situation.

"He had no family," Tillman huffed. "He was a loner, a brilliant mind, but he kept to himself."

"He had a family. A boy. Tandor knew," Case argued. "Somehow, Tandor knew. Tandor would've used him as a bargaining chip at some point, but he died before he could do it."

Tillman scratched the stubble along his jaw. "Well, then that just proves Robert was smarter than the rest of us. But not smart enough to avoid what Albert had in store for him. Robert was too focused on fixing his mother. That's all he wanted in life. He was the one who convinced his deranged father to start the medi-pod program. He was certain that, given enough time and with the brightest minds left in the city working on it, he could somehow help her. When Brock died, and Marty left with everything, it was over for Robert. Not so smart in the end."

"But as of last night, Albert believed Brock was still alive," I said, refraining from telling him how we acquired that information. "You kept Brock Shannon's death a secret."

"Of course we kept it a fucking secret," Tillman snarled, fists clenching and unclenching. "It was the only thing we had to keep that group in line. It gave them the *illusion* they were in control, taking orders from Brock. Albert and his cronies were in charge of the militia—had them hyped up on a constant salvation-and-sunshine diet. There could've been a rebellion if they'd learned Brock had died, so we had to keep that shit tamped down."

"Sounds exhausting," I said, faking a yawn. "All those lies, all that deceit. And for what? So you end up here in a clearing, dying in spectacular fashion with nothing to show for yourself?" It was big talk, seeing as how the man had to give only one command to blow us up from above. "What's in it for you? Why do your father's bidding for all these years?"

He took an angry step forward. "Salvation will be *mine.* I'm the only one who is equipped to lead the world into a new era." He thumped his chest, the sound reverberating in my ears. "Yeah, maybe the sun won't shine and all that other bullshit they told us for years, but I've got resources nobody knows about. My father had the wherewithal to hide them well. You see, my father was a devoted employee to Martin Bancroft. Martin trusted him, made him sign an oath, gave him riches beyond belief. My father was wealthy. He honored his agreement and spent his entire fucking life guarding Martin's assets. When Martin became Brock and lost his mind, my father was the *only* one who knew what the man really owned. Brock died in my father's arms. After that, the Tillman family rose to power. This is our legacy now."

I couldn't help it. I burst out laughing. "You've got

to be kidding me. That's *it*? That's your entire story? Martin trusted your father, made him a rich man, and your father turned his back on Martin's family? That's your honor? That's your legacy?" I gestured to Case. "Brock's living, breathing heir is standing right here, and you have the gall to tell him that nothing belongs to him, that it's magically all yours now? Without Martin, you wouldn't even exist. Your father probably would've died along with the rest of the population."

"It's mine by eminent domain." Tillman's face turned a ruddy red as he seethed. "I guard it. I'm its keeper. It's mine. I don't care if the blood in your veins is the same as his. This has nothing to do with you anymore. The world will be better off with me running things."

"I couldn't care less about me. But what about Robert's son?" Case questioned. "By the tone of your story, you had affection for Robert. Robert's son shares the same blood as your father's employer, the same one he swore to protect. By rights, everything you own is his."

Tillman appeared flustered, and then anger overtook him again. "Stop trying to confuse me," he commanded. "It won't work. I told you, Robert didn't *have* a family. Whoever you think that kid is, he's not Robert's."

Daze was Robert's son, and we had proof. Not definitive proof, but I'd take Maisie's word for it.

"I owe nothing to anyone," Tillman continued. "Once you're dead, this is all over and done with."

"And then what?" Bender asked. "You're just gonna march up to the city and take over? Kill everyone you don't like? Wait for the Flotilla to show up, so Marty can assume his position as leader?"

"Yes, we're taking over," Tillman answered. "Marty has no power any longer. I've been planning for this my entire life. Waiting on those old bastards to figure themselves out or die of old age was excruciating. Then Dixon got in the way. But now we're all set. We control the city, and once we're installed as the leaders, we summon Marty back with agreed-upon terms, and if he tries to interfere, he dies."

Wait, what?

I sputtered, "You're saying…that Marty is alive and the Flotilla is actually thriving and you're in contact with them?" That was the only way he could *summon* them.

But it couldn't be true. There was no way.

"Of course he survived," Tillman retorted. "Before the meteor strikes, Brock Shannon, aka Martin Bancroft, invested heavily in aquatic farming. The Flotilla wasn't just ships and supplies." He smirked, knowing we had no idea what he was talking about. "They rendezvoused with a ten-thousand-hectare farming community that Martin launched a year before the strikes. He located them in an area that his scientists assured him would have the greatest chance of survival. Islands called the Bahamas, or something like that. And it worked—it *fucking* worked." Tillman laughed. It was a nauseating sound. "Marty's been cultivating that area for thirty-some years. He's wanted to come back, but Albert convinced him it wasn't safe, that if he came now, he'd be killed."

This information was almost too much to process.

Not only had Case been lied to his entire life, but so had the entire population of the city—save for the Bureau of Truth. Marty had handpicked the elite and the smartest, knowing that he was taking them to a safe haven when he launched the Flotilla. A community had already been stationed safely and, from the sounds of it, had prospered.

I gripped my upper arms to try to keep myself rooted in place. I was furious. We lived in a ravaged world because these men had decided who would thrive and who would suffer in the aftermath of the meteor. Unfair didn't come close. It was a travesty. A slight on mankind. Greed had continued to thrive in our world, right under our noses.

"Are you saying my father is *alive*?" Case said through a clenched jaw. "That he's on some aquatic farm living happily?"

"I wouldn't say he's *happy*, per se," Tillman answered, chuckling. "They've gone through some tough times. Controlling the weather is impossible, as you know. They've been ravaged by a few storms. But for the most part"—Tillman shrugged—"things have worked out. Recently, though, I've heard some horror stories. People have gotten a hold of our communication system and screamed for help. Lots of torture, it sounds like. People thrown overboard, forced labor, you know, that kind of thing. Your father has always been a son of a bitch. He was going to succeed no matter the cost, and it looks like he did. Now he wants to come back and retire. I don't really blame him. It must be exhausting work out there. As long as he relinquishes what he brings back, we'll have no trouble."

My hands landed on the top of my helmet. My brain having trouble processing all this.

The Flotilla existed, and Case's father was a madman.

"Where are all these secret resources you're hoarding?" Bender asked. "The ones that don't belong to you."

"Like I'm going to reveal all my secrets." Tillman snorted. "I'm only being kind and generous to you in your last moments on earth. I can't lie—the looks on your faces are fucking priceless. It's like I hit you over the head with a graphene stick and made your brains glitch up. The world you thought you knew doesn't look quite the same, does it? Bender's crew thought they knew everything, but you didn't know *shit.* It's too bad, since at one time or another, you would've been considered assets. You could've worked for me and survived this mess. Too bad it didn't turn out that way."

"Me, take orders from you?" This time, it was Bender who threw his head back and laughed. It was full-throated and rich. "You have to be out of your mind. What you've done all these years is criminal. You have things in your possession that could've made this world a better place. Then, by the time Marty came back, you could've built a fucking empire. Instead, you greedy bastards screwed it up. You fought with each other like squabbling children. You know the real reason you haven't implemented your amazing scheme? You're scared shitless." Bender jabbed his finger at Tillman. "You have no idea if it's going to work, and it's gonna be hard. You know there are more people just like us that will stand up to you. You're going to lose men, and for what? For Marty to come back and make your life a living hell? Face it, bravado is the only thing holding up that shell of yours. My guess is that's what your father thought, too. Never had faith in you, did he? Knew you were going to fuck it all up. Did you kill him? Or did you pitifully wait around until the old man died?"

Tillman quaked. Rage thrummed from his body. I'd goaded him, but Bender had just called him out.

"You have no idea what you're talking about," Tillman said as he stormed forward. "I've never known fear a day in my life. Everything standing in my way is gone." His gaze shot to Case. "Or will be soon. Too bad you won't be around to see me fulfill my father's dream—the one where *I* will be the one to rebuild the city." He stopped a few meters in front of us and jammed his fist in the air. Everything about him reeked of confidence. It was his time to shine, and whatever had happened in his past was over. He swiped his arm down, screaming to the sky, "Strike. Them. Down."

As the UACs darted into position, we all scrabbled for our weapons. Quick as a lightning strike during a pulse storm, tiny doors on the drones slid open and bright white light burst forward.

"Holly!" Case shouted, lunging toward me. Aiming at the closest UAC, I managed to squeeze the trigger before Case took us down, my heart thumping loudly as I watched my shot go wide.

Blasts hit the earth, exploding the dirt around us. Several screams followed. Then the sounds of bodies thudding to the ground.

As quickly as it started, it was over.

My face was buried in Case's shoulder. I took a breath in and out just to make sure I was alive. "Case," I whispered urgently, my hands caressing his back, searching for injuries. "Are you hit?"

"No," he murmured, his face in my hair. "I'm not sure why." He began to ease off of me.

My eyes slid shut. I didn't want to look. I didn't want to see the rest of my family dead.

"What the hell just happened?" Bender growled. "I thought we were all going to fry."

My eyes snapped open, my head turning toward his voice. "You aren't hit either?" I sat up quickly. "Where's Lockland?"

"I'm right here," he said from behind me. He'd tried to dive for cover.

We all stood.

In front of us, it was hard to tell what had happened. Tillman hadn't been shot only once. He'd been blown to smithereens. So had three of his soldiers. Hardly anything was left, except a ton of blood and a few scraps of material.

A lone man stood at the center of the clearing. Very slowly, he lifted the massive laser gun off of his shoulder and set it on the ground, raising his hands. "I won't harm you," he called.

I moved forward. "Did you make those UACs hit Tillman and the others instead of us?"

He shook his head. "No," he answered. "But I did kill this one." He gestured at a fallen soldier in front of him.

From out of the woods, a figure emerged.

Maisie.

Chapter 25

We were in the cave, out of the drizzle. "Tell us again," I instructed Maisie. Then I turned to the soldier, who'd told us his name was Hans Buckley, Buck for short. "Then I want to hear your explanation one more time, in detail."

I was having trouble making sense of everything that had gone on during the last hour. My brain kept suggesting to my subconscious that it was all a dream, even though the logical part of my brain knew it wasn't.

"The UACs were constructed with an AI-compatible open mainframe," Maisie answered. "I infiltrated their systems, turning their voice-recognition modules into interior-based code. When Tillman gave the order, I followed it, but I chose who to strike down." So, in essence, Maisie had hijacked the UACs.

If she hadn't, we'd all be dead.

"How did you know not to kill this one?" Lockland gestured at Buck.

"As Tillman gave the order, this soldier shot one of the others," Maisie answered. "Based upon that action, I determined that keeping him alive would be useful. Soldiers don't turn on one another unless circumstances are extreme."

"You can say that again," I muttered. When she began to repeat herself, I held up my hand. "That was just a figure of speech. Soldiers turning on one another is very serious. You made a good decision." I glanced at Buck. "Your turn."

The guy looked miserable. He sat with his head in his hands, his helmet discarded on the ground, his dark hair standing on end. "Tillman's father wasn't the only one who Martin Bancroft entrusted with his legacy," he started. "My father, Hans Sr., was another. There were six original overseers, but only three had children. Tillman and I were the only ones who survived into adulthood. I was a quiet kid who preferred to go unnoticed. I've deferred to Tillman my entire life because, up until recently, he was the best at doing his job. But you were right." He inclined his head toward Bender, though not meeting any of our eyes. "His father hated him. He always thought he was lacking, never thought he could get the job done. Nothing was ever good enough. Tillman's father went as far as to enlist another man who he'd been grooming to be the leader of the takeover. Someone named Hutch. Tillman tried to kill him, but the guy snuck out before he could."

Good ol' Hutch. That asshole had injected me with Plush, intending to use me as a sex slave. Hutch had some pretty unique ideas about how to take over the government. Once he'd escaped from Tillman's death sentence, he'd found his way to Tandor.

"That means Tillman's father was alive until recently," I commented.

Buck nodded, fingers massaging his temples. "He's missing. We're pretty sure Tillman killed him around the time you defeated that guy from the South, Tandor, but nobody knows for sure."

"This entire thing is a long, sordid tale." I paced past Julian, who sprang to his feet.

"Would you like to sit down?" Julian gestured toward the rickety chair he'd vacated. "Please take my seat. I'm happy to stand."

"Thanks for the offer, Julian," I told him. "But I prefer to walk. It keeps my blood flowing and prevents my anxiety from crushing my organs."

"Would you care for a refreshment?"

I chuckled, wondering what exactly he would offer me. He must be picking up on my anger and irritation. "No, thanks."

"Why would you stand against Tillman now?" Lockland asked Buck.

The man finally looked up, glancing at Case, slowly shaking his head. "I know you're not going to believe me, but this is the first time I've ever heard of your existence. I knew Dixon came around once in a while and that he had meetings with Tillman. But I had no idea why. When I saw you, and heard what Tillman said, I had no choice but to honor the agreement my father made with Martin Bancroft all those years ago. Martin was an extremely generous man before he lost his mind and became Brock Shannon. My father had nothing but respect for him. Martin was trying, in his own way, to do his best by the survivors of the apocalypse. He loved his wife and boys beyond reason. The only way he knew how to accomplish anything was by throwing coin at it. My father was a good man. He would never have made the agreement with Martin if he'd thought it would harm anyone. He was indebted to Martin for choosing to save his life by harboring him in one of his bunkers. I made the only decision I could, and here we are."

"It's lucky Maisie recognized your intent," I said. My emotions were still roiling fiercely, so much so that I had a hard time focusing. So much deception, so many lies, so many years wasted. Meanwhile, decent people lived lives devoid of any hope, with no prospects for a better future.

That all changed now.

"What about the remaining soldiers at Tillman's base, the ones separate from the militia headquarters?" Bender asked. "And how many survivors of the militia are there? Who are we going to have to fight to end this?"

And believe me, we were finishing it.

"There's not many of us left," Buck answered. "Tillman left ten to guard our home base. Ten others were sent to headquarters, and the rest went with him. I'm the only one left of that group. I wasn't at the headquarters when the LiveBot blew it up, but I know they took severe losses. It shouldn't be hard to contain anyone who's left. Once you capture the base, the men will follow you. They feared Tillman, and now that Albert's gone, they will look for new leadership. They have no other choice."

"What about all the other members of the Bureau of Truth? The ones who held government offices?" I asked.

"I didn't know them very well, but for the most part, they were just there to follow orders," Buck said. "Albert made fun of them continually. They'd been born into the militia ranks, so they did what they were told. Albert made sure to rotate the men and women in and out of the city on purpose, indoctrinating them at a young age to keep them in line. It's the only way the secret could be kept that long."

"What about the women and children Tillman kidnapped from the small tribe?" I asked. "Please tell me they're safe."

He nodded. "They're locked up at our base. Tillman was going to use them as bargaining chips if he needed to, but you guys didn't fall for it."

"You're going to need to take us there immediately," Bender said, his voice brooking no argument. "We take it over, and after that, we figure out the rest."

It was a solid plan.

My gaze landed on Case. If Buck was miserable, Case looked wrecked. I met Lockland's eyes. His concern was apparent. He nodded once as I instructed, "You guys go out and take care of the bodies, or what's left of them, and prepare the crafts. Case and I will be out in a few minutes."

Bender hauled Buck up, surprising the guy, who fumbled to pick up his helmet before Bender pushed him through the cave opening. "If you so much as blink out of line, you're a dead man," Bender told him, making sure Buck remained in fear for his life until we knew he was telling us the truth.

As Maisie prepared to leave, I told her, "Keep an eye on Buck. Monitor his heart rate and blood pressure. I want to know if he's lying."

"Will do," she asserted in a very humanlike way. She was amazing. Without her, we'd be dead. None of us was ever going to forget that.

"One more thing. I want to thank you for saving our lives," I told her. "I have no idea how many times I'm going to say that moving forward, but I want you to know I'm grateful. If you hadn't been here today, we wouldn't have survived."

Maisie produced a tentative smile, her eyes blinking downward, which was even more humanlike. "Actually, if my calculations are correct, you had a thirty-eight percent chance of defeating the UACs and taking Tillman down yourself. There was only one thing that lowered that percentage in the final outcome."

"What was that?" I asked curiously.

"Case reached for you instead of his weapon," she stated, then turned and left the cave.

I glanced at the man sitting alone. My insides constricted. I knelt beside him, taking his hand. "Case," I whispered. "Please look at me."

Very slowly, the outskirt raised his head. "My family is responsible for so many atrocities."

"What atrocities are you referring to, exactly?" I asked. "Yes, people died, but they would've died anyway. The way I see it, your grandfather was trying to make a difference. He prepared for the decimation of the world the best way he could, and what he left behind will help many. It wasn't his choice to keep the impending apocalypse a secret. That order had to have come from the government. He was in a tough spot."

"My grandfather might've been trying to help, in a totally misguided way, but what about my father? You heard what Tillman said. The Flotilla not only survived, it prospered, but at what cost? Torture? Forced labor? I can't even think about what's going on out there without wanting to destroy something."

"I get it. It makes me crazy, too," I said. I had to keep in mind I wasn't processing everything the way Case was, because I hadn't found out my relatives were involved in huge conspiracies. But I did understand on an emotional level where he was coming from. "How about if we try to look at it another way? Your grandfather left extremely valuable resources behind, ones that Tillman hoarded. With those, coupled with the knowledge Walt, Elond, and Nareen can bring, we have the potential to build the city back up and give its inhabitants hope—*real* hope. For the first time ever. A better future is not out of reach. We can't forget the awesome medi-pod that Daze's dad built. He's a hero. That means something. That also means you're Daze's blood relative. The kid is going to be beside himself when he hears the news."

"It sounds like Robert was the only good thing in the family," Case said miserably.

"We don't know that for sure, and we won't know anything until we get to the bottom of what's waiting for us out there." I gestured toward the exit.

Case's gaze settled on me. It held weight. "My entire life has been a lie."

I shook my head as I gripped his hand, pulling him up. "No. Your life is just your life. I never knew my father or grandfather, either. Bender never knew his. I have no idea if Lockland knew his. Your life went the only direction it could go. Your mom escaped. She fled with you in order to give you a better chance at survival. And in my eyes, she accomplished that. Your life inside the militia's cult would've been extremely difficult. There's no telling how you would've turned out. You, right here, the man you've become—that's the life you were supposed to live."

Case stood next to me, one hand on my waist. "I wish I remembered more about my mother. I only have a few lingering details. She had a good voice. She liked to sing. But I can't remember any of the lyrics. Her smile made me feel good."

"See? Those are good things," I said. "I'm certain your mother would be proud of you today. Now we have to go out there and finish this. Tillman's base should give us the remaining answers. We have to find out what he's been hoarding all these years."

Case nodded, seeming to come to terms with this as best he could. At least for the time being. "Whatever we discover is going to change everything."

We walked out of the cave together. "Everything has already changed. The moment I rescued that kid from the gorge, my life was turned upside down. I believe whatever we find at the end of this will set a completely new path—but it'll be a better one than we had before. If that happens, then all the upheaval, the pain, the near-death experiences, finding out that our government betrayed us—all of it will be worth it."

"I hope you're right," he said as we climbed the incline. "If the city has a chance to move forward, then it's true. Everything was worth it."

We stopped in front of the craft we'd flown here. Bender was riding in one of the soldier's crafts with Buck, Maisie in the backseat. The props were spinning. Lockland had Julian in the passenger seat of Tillman's X class. "Follow Bender," Lockland called. "We stay back while they land. Buck and Maisie are going in first. We follow after."

I nodded as I climbed into the pilot seat, and Case got into the passenger seat. As we took off, I glanced at the outskirt. "Are you ready for this?"

"If I say no?"

I chuckled. “That’s not exactly an option.”

“Then I’ll settle for yes, I’m ready…but only because you’re sitting here next to me.”

He said the last part almost too softly for me to hear.

Almost.

Chapter 26

Buck had proven himself to be faithful yet again. He'd entered the base with Maisie and had been forced to shoot four of the ten soldiers. The remaining six had been secured with e-cuffs and were awaiting our questioning.

We'd found Lea and Mimi and the children. They'd been locked away in safe quarters, with ample food and water. We promised to get them to safety as soon as we could. Transporting them all up to the city to reunite with Helena and Sampson would take time. They hadn't been overly shocked to hear of Freedom's death.

"Where are the rest of the supplies?" Bender asked. "This can't be all of it."

The storage area Buck had just opened was impressive, filled with A class weaponry—such as the large laser guns the soldiers had been toting—a few UACs, boxes of bombs, and other upgraded technology. But Bender was right that this couldn't be all of it.

Buck scratched his head. "I'm not sure," he said. "I haven't been back here in a few years. The last time I was, there was a lot more than this."

"That means Tillman has moved things around," I said. "He knew his father was grooming a new successor. He would've wanted to keep whatever he had out of Hutch's hands. But in Martin Bancroft's letter, the one Maisie read in the cave, it stated that the trillionaire had stocked various warehouses around the country. This is not even a fifth of the volume of a single warehouse."

"You're right," Buck said. "But this place is all I've had access to. I never saw anything else. My father never mentioned another location. But there's a chance that the goods have been moved around a few times. Tillman's father was a paranoid guy."

I walked out of the room and into a bigger space that was used as a mess hall for the soldiers. Several large tables, two cooling units, couches, and a couple of sleeping pods dotted the space.

Lockland followed me out. "It's time to question the remaining soldiers. They may know something."

"You do that," I said. "I want to take a look around. We know they've been in contact with the Flotilla. There's a big radio tower near here. I want to find the communications room." I beckoned to Maisie. "Scan the area and see if you come up with any technology emitting a radio signal. Buck already told us that several places were off-limits to the soldiers. My guess is one of those places is their communications center."

Maisie nodded, lights sparking behind her eyes.

Bender and Lockland left to question the soldiers. Case said, "This outpost seems on the small side to me. These living quarters are barely bigger than the barracks we use by the sea. Doesn't seem right that the supplies would be stored here. In Martin's letter, he mentioned warehouses that were fully stocked."

I glanced around. "You're probably right." It was hard not to be disappointed. "Since Buck has no direct knowledge, and Albert and Tillman are gone, we're going to have to follow any clues we can find until we locate the right place."

Maisie moved toward the door. "I detect radio signals coming from a room nearby."

We followed her down several twisty hallways until she stopped in front of a door and turned the handle. It was locked. I unholstered my Gem, thinking I'd blow the handle off, but Maisie lifted her foot and smashed the door in with the force of a hydro-bomb.

I raised my eyebrows, my lips tilting upward. "That was impressive. You made it look easy. Though, your legs are made of silica-filled titanium, so that gave you an advantage."

"I enjoy having advantages."

We entered the room.

The station was small. A few monitors and an old-looking switchboard sat on a small table. A pair of headphones lay nearby. Case took a seat and placed the headphones on his head. He toggled some of the switches, but he shook his head after a few seconds and took off the headphones. "Just a lot of static. From what I can tell, there are only a few channels, and nothing seems like it's set up to work over a long distance."

Wherever the Flotilla was, it was far away, and to receive that distant of a signal, the equipment would have to be high-tech. There'd also have to be some sort of indication of ongoing communication, such as logbooks or etch boards.

"This isn't the place," I said definitively. "I bet this is how they kept in contact with the militia headquarters. A quick, easy access point." I glanced around the spartan room. This base was where the soldiers and Tillman ate and slept, but this was not where they conducted business.

We made our way out, looking into a few more rooms as we went. Some contained sleeping pods and other furniture, while others appeared to be used for storing utilities. We passed an armory, but the weapons were not as impressive as those we'd seen in the room Buck had shown us.

We met up with Bender and Lockland in the main area. Both were shaking their heads. "The soldiers are all tight-lipped," Lockland said. "They're fearful and not ready to talk. It would take some invasive methods to get them to spill what they know. Either that, or Babble. But honestly, I don't think they know much. These are grunt workers. One of them confessed that they hardly ever left this building, and when they did, they only went to the militia headquarters."

"Do you think they'll follow our leadership?" I asked. "Or will that be a problem?"

"Hard to know," Bender answered. "A couple of them seemed like they'd follow us, but the majority seem to be hedging their loyalties. They witnessed Buck kill their compatriots, but I don't think any of them are convinced that Tillman or Albert are really gone. It's going to take some time."

I sat down at one of the tables, while Lockland walked to a cooling unit and took out a jug of water. "We have to figure out where Tillman carried out the important operations. It's definitely not here. I have a hard time believing it was at the militia headquarters. He'd want his own space, especially if he was hiding things."

"He was a sneaky bastard," Bender said. "The type to hide something out in the open to throw us off the scent."

"Yeah, the headquarters was too crowded," Case said. "Especially with all those LiveBots."

My hand hit the table as I stood. "That's it."

"What's it?" Lockland said, setting the water in front of us.

"The mecca," I said. "The militia headquarters is located inside a Manufacturing Mecca." I couldn't contain my glee. "It was part of a complex constructed around a huge mag-lev train station. In Martin's time, it would've been the perfect cover to bring in tons of supplies without raising any eyebrows. I didn't notice any buildings standing, but I was coming in at superspeed, focused completely on reaching my destination." I turned to Maisie. "Check your database. I want to know who invested in this particular mecca. It should be on file. Which buildings were owned by Bliss Corp or Martin Bancroft or both?"

"Accessing that information," Maisie said. "Bliss Corp is listed as the majority investor of that mecca, as well as two other locations on the East Coast. They leased out every building except two. After construction, one of the warehouses was sold to a private investor. The name on file is C.T. Bancroft."

"That has to be his wife, Chandra," I said. "Where's the location of that warehouse?"

"It's two kilometers west of the militia headquarters."

"You said they leased all but two buildings, one of which was sold. What happened to the other one?" Lockland asked.

"The other one is listed as a weapons-manufacturing plant owned and operated by Bliss Corp."

I grinned. "That has to be it. Martin Bancroft used his company to build a mecca, which he profited from while using two of the warehouses for his own purposes. If he was manufacturing weapons, and the building survived the strikes, the technology could still be operational." I couldn't allow myself to get too excited until we saw it with our own eyes. "Maisie, do you remember other buildings in the area when we arrived?"

"From our directional exit from the mag-lev tunnel, it would've been impossible to see them," she said. "They would have been behind us as we headed toward the headquarters."

"That's all great," Bender said, "but we can't just fly into that area until we know it's safe. Whoever's left is going to be guarding it fiercely. They had to have a hierarchy, and someone's in charge."

Buck, sitting off to the side, had remained quiet. I called to him. "Buck, you need to contact the headquarters from the communications room. We need to know what's going on."

He nodded as he stood. "I can do that, but they won't be familiar with me over there. I wasn't a communications operator."

"It doesn't matter," I assured him. "You know enough to get a message to them. We'll be listening in and will coach you on what to say. If they don't know Tillman and Albert are dead, don't mention it. In fact, let them think Tillman's on his way. After all, we have his craft."

The room wasn't big enough for all of us to enter, so Maisie and Julian waited in the hall. Bender stood just inside the doorjamb. The rest of us crowded inside. Buck sat at the table, headphones on. He was familiar enough with the channels to get the right bandwidth. He grabbed a small mic. "S17, it's Base," Buck said. "Come in."

Almost immediately, the static fell away and a voice crackled over the speaker. "Thank God, Base. It's about time," a man said, his voice filled with anxiety. "I gave up on calling you an hour ago. What's going on over there, and why aren't you here helping us? They bombed the entire fucking place. There's only a few of us left."

"We'll be there soon," Buck recited smoothly. "Tillman went after the perpetrators. We all just arrived back."

"I hope you blew them out of the sky. Those bastards deserve to die."

"Who's in charge of the LiveBots?" Buck asked. On the way into the room, Maisie had explained that if she could get physical access to the LiveBots, there was a possibility she could manually switch them off. Once we gained control, we could use them as guards for the rest of the survivors until we figured out who would ultimately change sides.

"What are you talking about?" The guy's voice radiated anger. "Who cares about the LiveBots? We were bombed. People are hurt. We need help!"

Buck let up on the transmit button. "I don't know what to tell him."

"Say this," I said. "'Tillman is heading to the warehouse to gather weapons. The bad guys haven't been defeated yet. In order to win this battle, he needs the LiveBots to fight,' unless this guy has a better option. He won't, though, because everyone who survived is injured."

Buck repeated what I'd said, and the guy responded, "There's only ten or so working LiveBots as far as I know. The rest were damaged. But I'll have Kelly bring them over. Then we need to be evaced up to the city, or people are going to *die*."

"Copy that," Buck said. "Tillman and two other crafts will be there in fifteen. Be ready."

After we locked up the soldiers, assured Lea and Mimi that things were going to be fine, we got into our crafts.

Headquarters was expecting us, but I was still unsure about what would happen. A significant number of things could still go wrong.

Lockland piloted Tillman's craft, Buck in the passenger seat and Maisie in the back. Bender and Julian followed, Case and I behind them.

Case was quiet. I glanced over. "Do you think we're going to find it?"

"I think there's a good chance," Case replied.

"Maisie said there were at least two other mecca locations on the East Coast. It would be a miracle if they're both standing, but if they are, it could be that nobody's discovered them yet."

"I was thinking the same thing," he said. "It seemed Martin Sr. was in touch with some talented scientists. If they knew the approximate trajectories of the meteor once it broke apart, it could be that they're still standing."

"It's amazing what money could buy back then," I muttered. "If your grandfather hadn't been a trillionaire, none of this would be happening. It's easy to be angry at someone in his position and disgusted by the greed, but without what he did, the city wouldn't stand a chance."

"That's true," Case commented. "But it's also true that good, decent people could've utilized these resources a long time ago."

"I can't imagine what happened right after the impact," I murmured. "The fear, the sorrow, the shock. It's amazing people rallied at all. They could've all just curled up and died. The history that was recorded after the meteor strikes indicates that only ten thousand people survived, a few thousand more filtering in from other areas. That's nothing compared to what the population was back then. Every major city was brimming with millions of people. And the survivors weren't all rich like your grandfather, but thanks to his careful planning, their legacy will get hope for a new and improved future."

Case turned to me, smiling. "You sound like you're a supporter of my grandfather."

I chuckled. "I wouldn't classify myself as a supporter. After all, he lost his mind and killed people." We couldn't ignore what our history said about Brock Shannon and how he was a convicted murderer. "But he loved his wife and children enough to try to make the aftermath of destruction a better place for them. I can't imagine the pressure your father felt going through the apocalypse at seven years old, losing his mother to Plush, watching his father go crazy, all while trying to take care of his baby brother. It must've been upsetting and confusing."

"Each and every one of our lives is upsetting and confusing. That doesn't excuse a cruel man who chose to hoard resources that could have helped thousands. My father literally took everything he could and set out to rendezvous with an aquatic farm that was waiting for him."

I eyed Case. "You said you remembered a man visiting a few times, and you thought his name was Morty. Do you think it was your dad, Marty? Was he coming to say goodbye?"

Case shrugged. "I have no idea. Could be. Like I said, it was more like a dream than reality. But I'm glad he didn't take me along."

"We won't know the truth until we locate him."

Case shot me a look. "What do you mean *locate him*?"

"If the Flotilla exists, we'll find it."

Chapter 27

My tech phone went off. Lockland's voice came over the line. "We're okayed to land. Maisie has everything under control. I'm beginning to wonder what we ever did without this LiveBot."

"She's not a LiveBot," I answered with the speaker to my lips. "She's a military-grade status reader come to life. And I'm pretty sure she's the best thing that has ever happened to us. We'll be down in a minute."

I set down between two warehouses. Both buildings were intact and situated less than twenty meters apart. We entered the building on the right, where we found ten retail bots lined up in a row, heads bowed, apparently deactivated. Behind them, three men had been detained by Maisie and Buck. Two of them were out cold. The third looked petrified.

The building was massive—and mostly *empty*.

I walked over to Bender. "There's nothing here."

"Lockland went next door to check that building.

That's where they were making the weapons. This is the warehouse that was in the name of C.T. Bancroft, according to Maisie."

Case said, "Maybe Tillman was toying with us and my father took every last resource with him. Tillman pretended he had the goods, to inflate himself and his cause."

"No, I don't think so," I said, walking into the middle of the cavernous room. "He was too confident. Your grandfather was well prepared. And Tillman's father was paranoid. We're just not searching in the right place."

Lockland came through the door, and Maisie followed. "The other warehouse is impressive," he said. "The machinery hasn't been active in years, but I think we can get it operational if we find enough scrap metal."

"Did you find a stockpile of resources behind the machines?" I asked hopefully.

He shook his head. "No."

"Maisie, scan the general area," I said. "What are we missing?"

"I've already taken a preliminary scan of the grounds and have found nothing of interest," she replied.

I spun in a circle. "I refuse to believe this is it."

Case walked toward the back. A few pallets filled with boxes of protein flakes, storage containers, and such were scattered around. But Maisie was right, there was nothing here. Case placed his hand above his head. "What's behind this wall, Maisie?" he called.

"Oxygen and nitrogen," she answered. "The wall is

no more than twelve millimeters thick, constructed of steel, cellulose, wood pulp, and concrete. Air occupies the other side."

As I paced around the room, I tried to ignore the freaky retail bots lined up with their heads down. If they all woke up right now, would they attack? "What about below?" I stomped my boot on the ground. No ominous sound echoed upward.

"There is just earth below," Maisie said.

"Dammit," I swore. "I was sure we'd find something here. Tillman has to have a secret storage area someplace, and wherever it is, it has to be big enough to hold a lot of stuff."

As I passed by, Julian stepped forward, smiling. "Can I offer you a refreshment?" His hands opened in a welcoming gesture, like he had a bunch of treats just around the corner that he could present to me, if only I'd take him up on it. He was clearly adept at trying to calm a frustrated customer. He was reading my body language correctly. I *was* frustrated. Unfortunately for him, this wasn't the right setting for him to fulfill his preprogrammed solutions. "I would love to show you more merchandise," he continued, "but our latest shipment has been delayed. We're waiting for those pesky trains, but they should arrive any minute. Once they do, you will have many things to choose from. Until then, may I bring you a beverage? Perhaps a light snack?"

I stopped, my eyes widening.

Bender pushed off the wall where he'd been resting,

arms crossed. "What? I know that look. What the hell is it?"

"The mag-lev tunnels," I whispered. "They're huge. They're protected. They're almost in plain sight. I never had Maisie scan the area." My voice rose several octaves as I made my way to the door. "When we landed, she was busy obstructing the radio frequency. I headed into the first tunnel that looked clear, but I never checked the other five." I nodded as I spoke, putting the pieces together. "That has to be it. If those mag-lev trains were docked when disaster struck, they'd make the perfect storage containers."

"Where are the tunnels?" Lockland asked.

"I believe they're between here and headquarters, just east," I said, glancing at Maisie. "Maybe two or three kilometers."

"Holly is correct," Maisie said. "I am initiating a scan now. I detect four cargo trains inside the tunnels."

"Well?" I asked, not feeling at all patient, my hand turning the handle, ready to investigate. "Are they empty or full?"

"Their mass indicates they are full."

Chapter 28

"I'm not sure you should've left Reed in charge," Darby said. "I mean, *Reed*?"

"Reed is not in charge," I countered. "Buck is in charge. Reed is his second. And I don't know why you're complaining. Julian reports back to you every day, and he's in charge of the other retail bots, which means you're basically in command of eleven LiveBots. That has to be a dream come true. By the way, they're doing an awesome job transferring all the stuff to the warehouse so we can sort through it in a couple weeks. The other day they unpacked five industrial-sized bio-printers. There might even be more. Walt is ecstatic." The trains were overflowing with supplies. Each was more than twenty meters long.

"What am I?" Walt asked as he shuffled in, smiling. He'd set up his lab across from Darby's in the Emporium. We'd given him a choice of locations, and he'd picked here. I was glad, since I enjoyed seeing him every day. Elond and Nareen had taken over the smaller lab, originally set up by Tandor. We were still in the process of shuttling Walt's supplies up here, but he had a majority of his things now.

"You're excited that the retail bots unpacked five bio-printers yesterday," I reminded him. The goods thus far had ranged from basic utilitarian cooking supplies, to high-tech supercomputers. At least two picos had been discovered, which were amazing finds.

The task of getting everything sorted would take at least another month.

"Yes, that's great," Walt said enthusiastically. "The more to work with, the better. Feeding everyone in the city will take a lot of printing power."

After we'd found the cache Tillman had hidden, it'd taken us a week to sort through the survivors, determine their loyalties, mostly by giving them Babble, and transport them to safer accommodations, since the headquarters had been mostly demolished.

We'd even rushed two of them up to the city, because their injuries were critical.

There were thirty-three survivors in all, not counting the bots.

"I still don't think Reed is the right choice," Darby muttered. "That guy has been indoctrinated with an agenda counter to ours since birth."

"I know, you'd think he'd be the wrong one for the job," I agreed. "But the guy had a complete breakdown in front of me. The majority of the people down there were skeptics, and the relief of being set free was overwhelming. Plus, they have no access to weapons, and we only left one craft. They have nowhere to go. And we've informed them that they have to earn our trust in order to move up here. That's the deal." I had no doubt most of them would.

Case entered the lab, trailed by Daze. Both were smiling. It was a common occurrence around here. To say the kid was happy to discover Case was his blood relative was an understatement. Daze was ecstatic—he'd passed excitement and dived straight into mad love—and had barely left Case's side since we'd returned home.

"Claire just called," Case said. "She wants us. They think they might have something."

My eyebrows rose. "Already?"

He nodded. "The craft is waiting. Lockland and Bender are meeting us."

Daze hopped up and down. "I was there. I heard it. It was a girl's voice. She sounded sad."

I nodded to Darby. "Join us. You're not going to want to miss this."

Walt headed back to his lab room, tossing up a wave behind him, calling, "I'll be here if you need me." Walt was in charge of reworking the entire city bio-printing system. It was a huge job, but he was up for it. In fact, he was eager and willing.

The world would be forever changed by his cupcakes.

The trip from the Emporium to the Bureau of Truth's government building, which had been taken over by the loyalists—who weren't really loyalists anymore, since they were now the ruling party—took less than ten minutes.

"Madam President, you summoned us?" I chuckled as I walked in.

"Don't call me that." Claire made a sound in the back of her throat as she drew me in for a small embrace.

As she let me go, I replied, "Why not? It's your title, after all."

"No, it's not," she replied, flustered. "There was one informal vote. Nothing's official. One step at a time."

When we'd arrived in the city three weeks ago with the news of the scientists and all the newly uncovered resources, the government convened several emergency meetings. Claire was the overwhelming choice to take the helm. The job of ushering every inhabitant in the city into a new era would be a big one, but everybody knew Claire was the exact right choice.

"Whatever," I said. "What've you got?"

She led us down the hallway. "We found out they used a room on the top floor to communicate with the Flotilla. The connections are extremely spotty. It took us until yesterday to figure out all the signals and home in on the right one. Without Maisie, it would've been impossible."

"What's possible these days *without* Maisie?"

Maisie was the most important key to moving everything in the right direction. She had a database full of forgotten knowledge, combined with the ability to scan and triangulate things in a way that no human could ever do. She was a walking, talking supercomputer.

She was just what the city needed.

On our way to the stairs, which would lead us to the fourth floor, the door to the basement banged open, and Mary and Ned came through. I smiled. "How's it going down there?"

Mary gave me a bright smile, hugging me. "We've cured another fifteen this week. Claire has decided to open the Housing Division again, so we can find them suitable homes. We can't thank you enough, Claire." Mary's eyes sparked with excitement. She'd happily taken on what we were referring to as the Seeker Rehabilitation Program (SRP).

"It was the right thing to do," Claire said. "With the influx of the people from down South, as well as the seekers, everybody's going to need a place to live out of the rain. I have people on the streets investigating suitable residences right this minute."

"That's terrific," I said.

"It's all thanks to you," Mary said.

I shook my head adamantly. Since I'd been the one to take the trip down to the militia headquarters, and ultimately given Maisie a body, people had been attributing our success to me alone. "No, it's taken all of us to get this far."

Bender, Lockland, and Knox entered the front door behind us, Bender's voice booming, "Did we miss it?"

"No," Darby answered. "We're just on our way up now."

We said our goodbyes to Ned and Mary and continued to the fourth floor.

The room wasn't big, so the two people monitoring the communications got up and exited as Case and I sat, the rest filling in around us, Daze sneaking up front. Claire bent over, switching a lever. "It's just a recording," she said. "We've been trying to contact her for the last few hours, but she hasn't responded."

Crackling and popping noises issued out of the monitor's integrated speakers.

The voice was breathy and urgent. "Is anyone out there? We desperately need your help." The girl's voice was strong, but agitated. "This is Alaria. Things are about to get dangerous. We're trying, but we can't stop the tide. We're talking full annihilation if the bastard gets his way. People are going to *die.* Do you hear me? It's a scheduled extermination of our people. Please help us."

Interference came across the line, then a young man's voice yelled in the background, "I told you it wasn't safe. Ari, run!"

The recording clicked off.

I hit the switch. We all listened again with rapt attention.

"See? I told you she sounded sad," Daze said.

"Clearly, shit is going down at the Flotilla," Bender said. "The question is what are we going to do about it?"

I eased my helmet off, running a hand through my hair. "We have no idea where they are. We haven't been able to find any real coordinates. Two men from the headquarters made mention of a place called the Bahamas, but according to old maps and Maisie's database, that's a large area, and we don't know if that's actually where they are. We need to get her back on the line."

"My people will keep trying to make contact," Claire said. "But it sounds to me like she was somewhere she shouldn't be, and we're not going to get a hold of her again."

"I think we should try a different tactic," Case said. "We need to make this sound like an official call. Like the city is trying to get hold of whoever's in charge of the Flotilla—namely, Marty, if he's still alive. Then we go from there."

I nodded. "We don't bring up Alaria at all. Tillman said something about Marty wanting to come home. We act like we have news. That Albert has achieved the long-awaited takeover or something close. That is, until we find out exactly where they are."

"Then we go," Lockland said.

"Damn right we do." I stood, my chair scraping backward.

"If they need our help, we get there," Bender added.

"Preventing the annihilation of a population is our number-one goal," Darby said.

I settled a hand on Daze's shoulder. "There will be no extermination if we can help it."

Sneak Peek of

DANGER'S FATE

A HOLLY DANGER NOVEL:
BOOK SIX

AMANDA CARLSON

PART ONE: HOLLY

Chapter 1

"It's been a week since we've heard from her," I said. "We can't wait much longer, or there's a risk they'll all be dead." We sat in the main area of the Emporium, discussing what to do about the SOS call that had come from the Flotilla seven days ago today, from a girl named Ari. We hadn't heard from her since and nobody from the Flotilla was answering our calls.

Case stood against the wall, Bender straddled a chair, Lockland perched at the edge of a couch, and Daze and Darby sat on the ground, Daze's shoulder pressed up against my leg, as I sat on the couch opposite Lockland. Knox would've been with us, but he'd gone back down South to facilitate the transfer of the resources we'd uncovered. Tillman's stash had been huge. The LiveBots were almost finished moving the goods from the mag-lev trains to the warehouse. They'd done it in much less time than any human could've, and once it was all finished, we would go down and inventory the items, bringing them up to the city based on order of importance.

"Claire doesn't want us to move unless we can find the exact coordinates," Bender said. Claire was in Government Square, along with Maisie, figuring out her new role as our new president. She'd been the overwhelming choice to serve the city once we'd arrived back, and she was doing a hell of a job. She'd reopened the Housing Division, was overseeing the Seeker Rehabilitation Program (SRP), which had already saved twenty-nine individuals. She was working on a new Food Dispensary system, headed by Walt. The improvements to the city were happening quickly, and the population had reacted with enthusiasm. "It makes sense," Bender continued, "since none of us have experience taking a craft over the sea for a long period of time. We'd be flying blind, with no place to land and recharge. It would be a dumb-ass move to head out without knowing where it was."

"Based on what some of the militia members, who have had contact with the Flotilla in the past, have said," I argued, "we should be able to get within a twenty-kilometer range. It's an area called the Bahamas. Maisie has a detailed map in her database, and she's already cross-checked a likely location. A sheltered spot between two of the islands. We haven't checked the tech table at the barracks, but it could have one too. I think waiting is a mistake. You heard that girl. They're planning a mass extinction of their people. If we don't act, who knows how many will die."

Lockland stood and began to pace. "I understand the necessity of acting quickly, but Bender and Claire are right. It's dangerous to go in without understanding what we're getting into or where this place is. The ocean is dangerous and unpredictable."

"We have Maisie," I countered. "Just like I've been saying all week, Case and I can head out with Maisie, scope the location, and gather all the intel we need. Tillman's X class dronecraft"—which I had commandeered as my own, and had renamed Tilly in a bout of morbid irony—"is crazy loaded. It's got a working dash with a visual flight recorder and a superb distance radar. That, coupled with Maisie's expertise, and we have nothing to worry about. We can get out there, see what was going on, and come back."

"We give it one more week," Lockland said. Before I could protest again, he lifted his hand. "Do as much research as you can, draw up the maps, talk to the militia folks again, and get back to us. I give you my word you can move by then, even if we don't hear from the Flotilla."

"By *us*, you're referring to you and Claire, right?" I stood, settling my hands on my hips. Claire had pretty much installed Lockland as her second in command, without officially announcing it. It was a good choice, but it was beginning to interfere with our group dynamic. "I shouldn't have to say this, but our group and the government are separate entities. We've always worked apart. I'm all for involving them when need be, and I love Claire like a sister, but what we decide to do isn't up to them. It's up to us."

"Things have changed," Lockland said, a hint of weariness in his voice. "Now that Claire is in charge, and we're all playing a prominent role in the restructuring of the city, we have a larger body to contend with."

My head began to shake slowly back and forth, my expression set, hands still settled on my hips.

Case pushed off the wall, sensing my mood. "We don't have to decide anything yet," he said, his gaze flashing to mine. "Waiting a week is doable. We can handle it. More research needs to be done anyway. We want to go in with as much information as we can gather."

I was about to speak and tell Lockland exactly how I felt about needing a government approval, when Daze scrambled up from his position next to me. "I want to go, too," he pleaded. "I never thought the Flotilla was real. Now that we know it is, it's going to be so cool to see. Maisie showed me pictures of farms on water. They look like spaceships, with big bubbles on top, and another bubble on the bottom." He mimicked the shape of a globe with his hands. He was right. Maisie had been able to show us varying styles of aquatic farming that had been popular right before the meteor struck, as well as how our ancestors had viewed space travel by aliens. The two were remarkably similar.

Although, we had no idea what the extravagant trillionaire, and owner of Bliss Corp, who was also Case's and Daze's grandfather, Martin Bancroft, a.k.a. Brock Shannon, had actually purchased when he'd acquired a ten thousand hectare aquatic farming community, we had a pretty good idea.

The individual structures were watertight and buoyant, designed to flex and move softly under the rocking waves. Each unit, called an atlas, were sized for either a single-family or a multifamily, and provided separate sleeping areas, a common room, and waste room below the waterline, and a kitchen and large living area above the waves.

From what we'd been able to discern, each atlas had a massive, spherical deck, encompassing the entire circumference, at least four to five meters wide, with slotted spaces that allowed seaweed to grow beneath, which they harvested and ate, along with a variety of other things. A dozen atlases were tethered to a large Habitat, which mimicked a terrarium atmosphere, and was used as a communal meeting place, and also the place where they grew fruits and vegetables.

The only thing missing in this scenario was sunlight.

But according to the militia members, Martin Bancroft had anticipated this, and had installed special UV lighting in all the Habitats. Whether or not that was true, or if it had worked, wouldn't be determined until we arrived and saw for ourselves.

That was the farming community alone, and

discounted all the ships and supplies that had left with Marty, Martin Bancroft's son and Case's father, from our harbor thirty years ago. How it all fit together was a mystery.

I smiled at Daze, momentarily forgetting my irritation with Lockland. "You can't come on the first run, because everything's unknown, which makes it dangerous. Once things are stabilized, I'm sure we'll go back and forth a few times."

"You're not scared of danger," Daze said knowingly. "After all, it's your name."

I chuckled, glancing up to meet Lockland's gaze. "It is my name. But that doesn't mean I'm not scared. It just means helping out Ari and her people is the right thing to do."

Bender grunted, sensing what was coming next. He rose off the chair, sliding it out of the way with a loud scrap. "One week. Whatever Holly finds, we go with it." As he spoke, his eyes locked with Lockland. We all knew this was a slippery slope, him and Claire being immersed in the government, one that we were going to have to navigate whether we liked it or not.

Things were changing now, even quicker than before.

Claire's position was accepted by most, but not all.

Everyone was relieved that the Bureau of Truth hadn't succeeded in their coup to overthrow the government. But not everyone felt like we were heading in the exact right direction. There'd been some grumbling.

Lockland looked as if he was going to say something, but changed his mind. He brought his head down. "One week."

~

DANGER'S FATE will be available soon! Don't miss out on the next adventures of Holly & her crew. To keep up with all my releases, please visit my website and sign-up for my newsletter. Happy reading!

NOTHING IS CREATED WITHOUT A GREAT TEAM.

My thanks to:

Awesome Cover design: Damonza.com

Digital and print formatting: Author E.M.S

Copyedits/proofs: Joyce Lamb

Final proof: Marlene Engel

ABOUT THE AUTHOR

Amanda Carlson is a graduate of the University of Minnesota, with a BA in both Speech and Hearing Science & Child Development. She went on to get an A.A.S in Sign Language Interpreting and worked as an interpreter until her first child was born. She's the author of the high octane Jessica McClain urban fantasy series published by Orbit, the Sin City Collectors paranormal romance series, the contemporary fantasy Phoebe Meadows series, and the futuristic/dystopian Holly Danger series. Look for these books in stores everywhere. She lives in Minneapolis with her husband and three kids.

Find her all over social media

Website: amandacarlson.com
Facebook: facebook.com/authoramandacarlson
Twitter: @amandaccarlson
Instagram: @author_amanda

CPSIA information can be obtained
at www.ICGtesting.com
Printed in the USA
LVHW111656190220
647495LV00005B/1000

9 781986 387903